THE TALOSITE

D1295126

ALSO BY REBECCA CAMPBELL

Arboreality

The Paradise Engine

THE TALOSITE

REBECCA CAMPBELL

Rebecca Campbell.

UNDERTOW
PUBLICATIONS

THE TALOSITE

Copyright © 2022 by Rebecca Campbell

Cover art by Yaroslav Gherzedovich

Cover design by Vince Haig

Interior cover art © Rawpixel

Interior design and layout by Michael Kelly

Proofreader: Carolyn Macdonell-Kelly

First edition

All rights reserved.

The publisher gratefully acknowledges the support of the Ontario Arts Council.

ONTARIO ARTS COUNCIL
CONSEIL DES ARTS DE L'ONTARIO
an Ontario government agency
un organisme du gouvernement de l'Ontario

Library and Archives Canada Cataloguing in Publication

ISBN: 978-1-988964-40-9

This book is a work of fiction. Any resemblance to actual events or persons is entirely coincidental.

Undertow Publications, Pickering ON, Canada

No part of this book may be reproduced in any form or by any electronic or mechanical means, including information storage and retrieval systems, without written permission from the publisher, except for the use of brief quotations in a book review.

Typeset in Athelas

Printed in Canada by Rapido Books

For Don

PRAISE FOR THE TALOSITE

"*The Talosite* is further proof Campbell is a supremely gifted writer. She's invented a strange, dark, compelling, and poignant alternative world in which the dead can be resurrected. An absolute must read!"

— PAULA GURAN, *YEAR'S BEST DARK FANTASY & HORROR*

"Campbell captures the perfect voice in this deftly crafted alternate history that explores wonders and horrors and the blurred space where they bleed into one."

— A.C. WISE, AUTHOR OF *THE GHOST SEQUENCES*

"An intricate false history of WWI, an emotional and stylish reimagining of Frankenstein and reanimation legends, *The Talosite* fixedly explores the unfathomability of both love and mass death."

— NABEN RUTHNUM, AUTHOR OF *HELPMEET*

La victoire avant tout sera
　　De bien voir au loin
　　De tout voir
　　De près
　　Et que tout ait un nom nouveau

— GUILLAUME APOLLINAIRE, "LA
VICTOIRE," 1917

PART I

AUTUMN 1916

1

NED

Ned's first thought was giant, like the giants of Potsdam that Franky had warned him about. Eight-foot Prussians. Kill you when they fall as much as when they jab you or shoot you through the eye. Marksmen, too, the advantage of height. Franky was a barrack room lecturer and often held forth as Ned listened, by turns shocked and amused by all the things he had not known about the world until he arrived in France the year before.

This Potsdam Giant stalked toward them, lit first by moonlight, then by flares.

"He must be seven feet tall," Franky said. "Look at the bugger. Seven feet?"

But what was he doing in the moonlight like that? A death wish.

"Bernard will get him, don't worry," Franky said.

Across the mud, German voices raised in admonition, then panic. "*Kommzuruck! Kommzuruck!*"

Halfway now. Taller and taller.

"Bernard has him," Franky said. "Eight feet? Is he eight?"

More shouting on the other side, and shuffling activity up and down the trench. In the moonlit shadows he could imagine a helmet raised, a scope. More shouting. Another flare.

Now the Giant was close enough to see a face beneath the helmet, or at least its lineaments. "More than eight feet," Franky said. "Is the blighter more than nine?"

Then Bernard, in his sniper's blind down the trench, did his duty. A ring, a ricochet. The Giant stumbled.

"Bernie!" Franky said. "Good lad. Good lad."

The Giant staggered up again, his arm limp. Still stalking fearlessly toward them.

"They're like locomotives, aren't they, giants. Too bad we don't have more like him. Need Irish giants. You know, the giant—"

—Another shot—

"—O'Brien. We want his kind. Could take a step—"

—Another shot. The Giant fell twenty feet from their position. Ned could make out the whole man's length. At least eight feet.

"—and be in the middle of that trench. Could stand up here and piss on their goddamn square heads. His cock was—" here he grunted and waggled his forearm obscenely.

Across the mud, the Germans had settled down, though Ned still sensed the same scurrying activity, the muttered grunts and gutturals, which he did not understand, but which he hated.

In that night's wiring party, he crept over the parapet and into the open, swampy world, as fear galvanized his skin and knotted his guts around his heart. He had a line of wire to cut east-north-east of their position, which took him within a few feet of the Giant. He wriggled over the lip of a shell hole, or perhaps the parapet of an earlier trench, or the body of a horse entangled with the wagon it had pulled to this place in 1914, before expiring in a shower of earth and shrapnel. Or it might be some ancient garden wall. One never knew. He looked down the slight incline to find the Giant closer than he had reckoned. His right arm sprawled toward Ned, naked and rotted and scarred, its skin pale and crossed by the white fuzz of decay far more advanced than he expected in one who had died the day before. He crept forward again, and by the light of flares could see the man's face.

Another flare and he thought the Giant twitched. For the first time in a week of bombardment, and the miserable wait for combat, Ned felt a new kind of fear. He told himself that flares and no-man's-land will do strange things to soldiers' eyes. But then the Giant twitched again.

He had to think: did one rescue the monstrous German stranger, or did one abandon him to the deepening mud?

He grabbed the Giant's arm and pulled, saying, "come on you bastard, come on. *Schnell!*"

Something snapped inside the German, and the arm tore loose at a kind of seam on the bicep, trailing tendons and muscle into the mud. The hand in Ned's hand stopped twitching. The body it had been attached to did not.

Then the whistle of a flare overhead, sparks descending. He pressed himself into the mud, still holding the disembodied hand, knowing that twenty feet away the Hun rose. The first shot. The second. He cursed the early education in self-sacrifice that had led him to reach his hand out to the Giant. He cursed the providence that had led him to this spot in the first place, and the war itself, as the Hun approached, faceless creepers as the flares continued their descent.

A spray of machine gun fire from the Canadians. Bernard. Franky. He willed himself to total stillness and in the darkness that followed the flare, he could not tell whether the German soldiers had crept back in their trench or were pressed, as he was, against the forsaken earth. Then someone was beside him, not Franky nor Bernard nor sarge: too clean to be one of theirs. The unusually clean man said, "may I?" and took the Giant's hand from his—he wasn't aware that he still held it—then shoved him back toward his trench.

THE GENTLEMAN who interviewed him at HQ was Captain Beauchamp. He was English, with a small moustache in the manner of English officers, and neither cap badge, nor insignia, though his buttons showed phoenixes. They sat at a bare table, requisitioned from some farmhouse, Ned guessed, tracing with his eyes the patina of bread-making and vegetable peels. "Now," said Captain Beauchamp, "You found the soldier dead the next day."

"Yessir. Or. No sir. In the flares it's hard to say. He'd been there two days. But I would swear I saw him twitch."

The man wrote a line in his gilt-edged notebook, asking Ned to repeat details. It was ten minutes before he could ask, "Did you get the Potsdam Giant?"

"The—what?"

"Potsdam Giant." He repeated. "What Franky called it, sir."

"Franky? Oh. Yes. Private Goble. We got what was

left of it. If we'd heard sooner, we would have had more. Rats are a problem."

Franky had lost his leg getting the Giant those fifteen feet back to the trench. Ned never saw him again. "What was he?" Ned corrected: "it?"

"A Potsdam Giant, obviously. Prussians are quite tall." Ned knew it was bunk, but the man had a posh accent and a neatly clipped blond moustache, and his hands were very brown and very clean. "We'll want you to talk to one of our clerks if you can be spared."

"Yessir," Ned said. That was a stupid way to put it. Everyone could be spared. No one could.

Still, it meant a few hour's quiet up the line. Not as far up the line as he had expected, though. They were in one of the large, sprawling villas outside Paris, out of range of the shelling, but not the noise. When he saw it at a distance, he thought it must be a casualty clearing station built around a villa of great beauty and decrepitude, though he could not say why the staff at a clearing station would be so interested in the Potsdam Giant. While he waited inside what had been a handsome foyer, he saw a girl, young-looking, in a patch of light at the end of the hallway. There was a halo of ginger around her head, and when he had drawn closer, he saw that her hair was green, and dark red, too. Her skin was a deep, buttercup yellow that he liked, though he did not often see it on a woman's face. He tipped his hat. She glanced at him then walked onward, a door snapping shut behind her.

When she was gone, he saw a filament catch the light, a long hair that hung from the door jam, reflecting green like verdigris. He caught it. Wondered. Dropped it. And then continued along the corridor where he had been sent, a small room requisitioned from the earlier inhabitants of the villa. He could see from the upper windows the treeless dark of no-man's-land, a smudge on the eastern horizon. Another table, from another farmhouse kitchen, where he repeated his story in greater detail, punctuated by further questions regarding the reaction of the German side of the trench, and the way the Giant moved. When the man's questions were exhausted, and Ned no closer to understanding what he'd seen, his interrogator paused.

"Do you think," he began, "that if you saw another —what did you say—Potsdam Giant—you would recognize it?" When Ned nodded, the man added, "What would you think of joining the stretcher bearers?"

"I don't know, sir."

"You'd be in a good position there, to keep watch for giants. You're no doubt aware of automata?"

"Yessir. I suppose, sir. But mostly in stories."

"The Hun have innovated. Improved on nature and made automata like your Giant, which are rather more useful in the battlefield than the old-fashioned kind. That one was the first we've captured alive, but there are more coming, and we need to find them. We are in need of eyes. Stretcher bearers make good eyes."

And so, through little effort and no design of his own, Edward Wallace's future was settled.

2

ANNE

In March 1916, Anne Markham was in Manchester, twenty-one and far from the home in London she had once shared with her father. Her fingernails had been brightly yellow, the colour of ducklings and daffodils. Her hair was green shot through with copper, which she considered an improvement on her usual pale brown. The new colour had come with her work in munitions and the interaction between keratin and trinitrotoluene, but the effect was so strange and spectacular that, on those rare occasions she looked in the mirror, she did not recognize the thin yellow creature she had become in her daily handling of TNT. Bomb-making was a job she had earned because her tiny, pointed fingers were clever at tiny, pointed tasks. Years of embroidery had given her skills she had not thought would be so useful during a global conflict, but this was total war and here she was, drinking tea in the early morning after her night's labour, while first shift workers streamed through the street outside. The tea was weak. The bun stale. She was not yet ready to sleep, though Millicent had left their bed by now, and it would still be warm with her nighttime perfume: *Quelques Fleurs* sprinkled over her chemise.

In the factory nearby, which Anne had so recently left, Millicent stepped into the still, hot room among the cordite and TNT, her hands as brilliantly yellow as Anne's, her hair red-gold. Someone somewhere struck a spark from the unseen nail in her shoe, or an unnoticed hair pin, and the inferno was instant, spreading outward so quickly that the neurological signals of pain and heat had not yet reached Millicent's brain when the shockwave blasted her bones. Her body evaporated.

The windows of the teashop shattered. With the broken glass came a new ringing in her ears that overwhelmed the sounds of the street. Outside, the crowd on the pavement stopped, looked up, then turned as one animal toward the factory gate. Joining them, Anne saw the familiar red smear of blood and her mind stopped, drifting in a slow-circulating spiral of a moment. Afterward, she could remember details: the broken bricks, the smashed teacup with the rose on it, the smudged blood drying where the girl's eyes had been blown away. But she couldn't have told anyone how long she had stood in the street, joining the crowd who excavated the factory in search of any survivors. Time must have passed. She must have walked home, because she found herself there at twilight, filthy, her fingernails broken.

That was six months ago, but the explosion still reverberated through her bones, as though it had not passed but happened in the war's eternal *now*, which in two years had already driven her from her home and the old, orderly life she had lived with her father.

Now it was September 1916 and she was in France, her skin still faintly yellow, but the green and copper hair falling from her scalp. There was only one mirror in the villa they had commandeered; she avoided it, wrapped a white scarf around her head and pared her nails down to stubs. Then she set her mind to the work that had brought her to France in the first place: the creation of automata from the fallen soldiers of the western front, following the principles she had learned while assisting her father, the eminent experimental neurologist, Henry Markham. As he had done, she revived the bodies of the fallen with copper wire, aethereal fluids, the filaments of the fungus Armillaria lazarites, and electricity. Each creature required a corpse inoculated with lazarites shortly after death, then a web of wire stitched beneath its skin. Then the sudden shock of faradaic current, and the piecemeal neurological network fused into something new. What arose was no longer a man, but now an automatic soldier, suited to tasks that required strength and nervelessness, but unable to operate an Enfield. She saw them often, hauling artillery over rough ground or digging trenches. Their new lives were short, but they worked without sleep or food or speech until they stopped suddenly and absolutely, even if one reapplied current and copper wire.

She was good at this god-like tatting. Their lab was close enough to the line she could hear fire most nights, a necessary risk when they needed fresh bodies daily. Based on their most recent orders, she guessed they wanted automata they could set to walking over no-man's-land, triggering mines to save a second and third and fiftieth wave of living troops. But as she worked, she often imagined other ways to fulfill the brief: perhaps squat creatures half the height of a man, creeping crab-wise, their femoral shafts replaced by steel, little Bosch demons scuttling through The Garden of Ordnance to the Garden of Combat. She had little luck building these more ambitious automata when the War Office wanted simple resuscitated bodies, and she had neither the time nor the resources to further her father's experiments.

The day after the Declaration, Father had offered his services to the War Office, outlining the possibilities for combat automata. He had wanted her to continue as his assistant, but in an unusual act of rebellion, she had insisted on her own war work. All through September 1914 she had written letters and requested positions while Father sulked, silent at the breakfast table, testing the nerve responses in each of his toes with needles and ice. He shook his head when she took up the familiar tools and tried to do the job that had been hers for years. Beneath the pall of his silence, she packed a small bag and left for munitions training. She wasn't there to look after him while his ankle healed from the sciatic procedure, which they'd undertaken together at the end of July. Despite the sulk, his letters had arrived regularly, more like reports than missives of fatherly affection, and she had kept them as records, still his secretary. When he wrote about an infection at the incision in his ankle, she left immediately, but he was dead before she arrived home.

Once, against Calloway's wishes, she'd shown Captain Beauchamp her drawings. Bodies made for trenches and infantry raids, bodies without auditory nerves, untroubled by bombardment, with low centres of gravity and many short limbs that would allow them to roll with each shell blast. She had thought that they might be armoured, too, following the principles of the tortoise or pangolin. She had drawn long centipede-creatures using the spines of horses and the heads of men.

He'd smiled tightly, looked over them and said, "whimsical."

"We could expand on father's research and make far more useful creatures—"

"—Miss Markham. After the war you'll no doubt work at St Bartholomew's, and whimsy will be rewarded. In the meantime, we need automata. As fast as you can, Miss Markham."

The whole war turned on bodies. How many one had. How many one could get. Using them twice was just good strategy. Wasting time on experimentation was not.

After he left, she had said to Calloway, "this can't be the best way to do it. There must be alternatives. Father would—"

"—this isn't St Bartholomew's," he'd said, irritated. Separated from his wife and young family, Calloway was intent only on staying as far away from the front line as the work allowed, and completing it as quickly as he could.

Anne was in France in 1916 for more than her tatting skills, and it was Calloway who had brought her there. After father died, and John at Neuve-Chapelle, and after Violet had lived her few weeks outside the womb, and Millicent in the factory, Anne was living in her father's house outside London in a state of numbness that reminded her of a cocaine block, her body no longer her own, though it continued to eat and sleep on a familiar schedule. It was raining again. She was stupefied with the heat and quiet of the house. When the doorbell rang she had thought, I won't answer it, I won't, but twenty-one years of training overtook her, and a rattle at the door meant the mail, and she stood, drank a glass of water from the stale carafe beside her, which she could not remember filling, and found a letter on the mat. On official letterhead, Dr. Stephen Calloway sought the expertise she had learned as Dr. Markham's assistant. The Doctor's neurological work, especially on animal electrical fluid and lazarites, automata, and the physiology of death, meant he was the tutelary spirit of Calloway's whole military enterprise, a collaboration with colleagues at the Université de Paris and Montpellier, magnificently named the Neurological Ingenieurs.

Calloway had been one of father's favourites, often at their house when she was a schoolgirl. He visited the next day in uniform, no cap badge or insignia, but his buttons had phoenixes. Together they ate the cake he brought and he told her about their work near the frontline, the mass production of automata, while their former German and Austrian colleagues did the same across the line. Outside the window, the garden was overgrown.

"You'll come, then," he concluded.

"No," she said. "Why? I can't do anything. I have to pull the dandelions."

He removed a set of notes from his case. She recognized the heading for father's last, uncompleted monograph, regarding the neurological effects of the trenches. "That's not Dr. Markham's hand," he said.

"I worked under his direction."

"We all work under his direction. He's dead and he's still our director."

Anne shook her head.

"You know what his work could mean for the war —damn it, Anne. Be a good girl."

She sent him away. But that night she couldn't sleep for hearing Violet's tiny cries, and John's last *never fear, duckling, I'll be home soon*, and the scent of Millicent's *Quelques fleurs*. She wrote her acquiescence before dawn, on the principle that those voices might stay behind on English soil, where they belonged, rather than following her to France. After everything that had happened, it was almost a relief to join Calloway's little regiment of Neurologists. She understood them, even if they wore khaki now, they reminded her painfully and pleasantly of her father, though she missed the German and Austrian men who had formed much of his lab at St Bartholomew's.

On receipt of her note, Calloway brought her to an undistinguished brick warehouse where the London Ingenieurs undertook their experiments.

The body that lay on the table was as undistinguished as the building. A boy, thin, his ribs showing knobbily through his skin, and his chest sunken, his chin pimpled and his nails ragged. He had died from a lymphatic infection, she guessed, based on the angry purplish wounds along his belly, now sprouting white tendrils of lazarites across the skin. Little white stitches that slowly overtook the wound, as they would soon overtake the boy's eyes and ears, until he was a skin bag, a flimsy bit of lace, left behind by the voracious and curious tendrils of lazarites.

Calloway had already threaded the brain with copper and run a wire down the spinal cord, the stitches large and loose.

"In the past," Calloway said from behind his batteries, "I suppose one would have incanted something, and waited for the lazarites to work. But one isn't a shaman."

"Father knew a Shaman in Siberia. They played chess by post. I wonder if they ever finished the last game. Father met him in Murmansk and demonstrated the resurrection of a Cossack who'd died of sepsis."

"Oh. I had forgotten about Vylka," Calloway said curtly, then did something to his glass batteries, luminous green under the raw light of day that poured in through the skylights at the top of the theatre. "Stand back," he said.

She waited. The medical students in khaki and phoenix buttons stopped their whispering. When Calloway connected the wires the air shattered. A crack. A shimmer of blue light around the body as the mycorrhizal threads of lazarites seemed to grow luminous and then fade again into the daylight and she could not tell if this was the secret webs grown incandescent as electricity flooded them, or if this was a throb in her eyes, the startled pulse of emergent tears.

They were so familiar, these young students with their redly shaved faces and too-large collars. She thought, father will just be a minute, to talk to us about the creature whose fingers now twitch on the board before us.

Calloway rushed from the batteries to the table. The man there jerked, trying to roll away, to stand, and she thought she could hear her father, somewhere, laughing, and she laughed too, to think of the mystery of it, no incantation, no unreliable strain of mould that might produce a monster or a berserker.

She was beside him, then, touching his startlingly cold hands, and helping him stand, though his dull eyes did not register her face. But she still laughed for now he took his first step in this new life, and then his second, stiff because of the rigour that had begun to set into his lower limbs. He staggered and fell. The others stood back, watching, and she knelt beside him and helped him stand. He shuffled after her, looking where she pointed. Docile, she led him toward the sunshine that poured in from the courtyard outside.

"That," she said to him, "is the sun. It will warm you."

He was beyond heat and cold, of course, beyond good and evil and hope and despair and love and hate. He was made of copper wire and electrical sparks and aethereal fluid and hyphae.

Behind her, they chattered. "What is it for?"

"Demonstration model. For the generals. A few

aren't properly convinced, though considering what the Hun are doing with autotmata, I'm surprised."

"Distasteful for old soldiers, I imagine. They're not used to experimental technology. Want everyone in red serge and infantry squares."

As she listened, she examined the incisions where Calloway had inserted wire beneath the skin, and the burn mark from the battery. Such clumsy work, she thought, I can do better.

WHEN CALLOWAY APPROACHED the War Office about recruiting her, he had said that she was suited to the work because of her peculiar education. He was right: she had been peculiarly educated. Her first surgery had been at fourteen, when she held the white enamel tray and the gauze while Dr. Schellenberg opened her father's left arm below the elbow and cut the ulnar branch of the medial cutaneous nerve. She had sutured the incision while Schellenberg observed, twenty-three perfect stitches along her father's forearm, held in good tension as she had been taught. She had removed the stitches two weeks later, but it had taken five years for sensation to return to his forearm. She had attended other such surgeries: on his right foot, his left thumb, each one expanding their knowledge of the human nervous system. His right hand had been the limit of experimentation: he needed it to write, and to dismantle cadavers in his quest to understand the destruction and regeneration of nerves.

After that first surgery, she drew the interior of his arm: the incision, the tourniquet, the tiny knots of her sutures pulling against the skin when he moved, so even after he had recovered his forearm was still dotted with tiny white puckers. If he had lived, there would have been only the faintest sketch on his skin to show the wound, and a monograph on the speed at which nerves re-grew. She had only been taught two stitches suitable for human skin: the double herring-bone; the French knot, both of which appeared on their tablecloths, made by some great grandmother she had never met. While she drank tea, she often wondered what that ancestral embroideress would think of what her skills had wrought.

Father taught her automata theory while he experimented on his own body and worked on pithiatic patients. At eighteen, she was the youngest of his students, allowed by reason of their relationship: it was a great man's indulgence, the others thought. Excessive paternal affection. But she was also his typist, and the one who made him tea. The painstaking expansion of neurological knowledge occupied their afternoons in the anatomy theatre, but in the evening, he told stories from the Haitian revolutions, the skirmishes of the Ohio River valley, the Maori Wars, where automata were common.

Automata, he had insisted, belong to an earlier age of man.

"We do not," he said, "torment flesh unnecessarily. We are better than that now. But."

But the mechanisms of resurrection were intriguing and revealed important truths about the nature of the human body. A neurologist could experiment on automata in a way one could not on a living man. Perhaps, one day, we may wake from our own deaths and find ourselves transformed.

As a child, her favourite book had been *Kunstformen der Natur,* by the German naturalist Ernst Haeckel, from which she had copied pictures. The book, or perhaps her careful recreation of its images, had revealed to her the order and pattern of the universe itself, in the segmented legs of insects and the roots of trees, the spreading networks of lichen over rock, and the skirts dropped from the *Phallus indusiatus,* the palmate river deltas and the branch capillaries of a leaf. Studying those lithographs, she felt that if her eyes opened a little wider, if her mind and pencil were better trained, she could grasp the beauty and order of all life and guess at the rules that governed it: the branching and the palmate, the divergent and the intersecting.

Father had nodded vigorously when she tried to explain it to him, and said, "Yes, yes my dear, a set of laws that applied to both mycelium and neuron. If we could only see how."

This had always been her father's gift, a voracious polymathy that consumed everything it encountered, all integrated with that capacious mind, sometimes a magpie, sometimes the branching filaments of mould transforming matter, or so he put it. He could discourse excitedly with mycologists and neurologists and etymologists, debate high churchmen and pagan revivalists on Mithraic cults, while teaching medical students the symptoms of stroke. In the life he led before her he had founded a dining club, and eaten barn owls and *Psilocybe hispanica*. He like vodka and gefilte fish and scorching chili peppers. He had dug up burial urns in Sardinia and studied painting for six months in Paris. It was not until he was twenty-three that he settled on his final career, and began the work that occupied the rest of his life: unpeeling layers of skin and bone and dural sheath to reveal the structures of the brain itself, the branching, multifarious pathways that run from the core of the self to the extremities, and reach toward the outer world.

During the long summer of his recovery after those first neurological experiments, he often spoke at length, sometimes in conversation, often dictation for his monographs. She remembered him under the cedar tree at the foot of the garden languid in the long, golden twilight, while she took down his words: "If one could find the common quality, the place where one system connects to the other, one would understand something essential about our lives on this planet, whether it is in the animal body or the mycological webs. Or the roots of trees. Until we understand the connections, automata will remain a natural curiosity. And true resurrection is no more than a dream."

Perhaps. Father was dead. Anne's only lover, John, was dead. Violet had hardly been alive, so brief were her weeks outside the womb. Millicent was dead, and a million others were dead when Calloway arrived with his cake and his possibilities. Her yellow hands had reached for her sewing basket, without thinking, the variety of silks available to her, and she remembered the dense tug of human skin beneath her needle. Father's skin. He had begun that work: perhaps she would have the opportunity to finish it.

BEAUCHAMP SENT word that a corporal had found one of the German automata near a Canadian trench. It had stopped moving by the time it reached her, but what she saw set her mind on fire. She and Calloway examined it in the basement of the villa, the only place they had a table large enough to support its huge frame. Unlike the other German automata she had seen, this creature was made of multiple bodies, at least three. The spine had been extended with metal and animal bones.

Calloway opened its pelvic cavity, and together

they traced the innovations on this new kind of automaton. "Vagus nerve," she muttered, drawing a hair-thin thread from the femoral sheath, slick with animal electrical fluid. She wound the wire around her ring finger and over her knuckle.

"What is it?"

"Platinum."

"Platinum?"

She tested it against her teeth. The taste of blood. "An alloy. Gold as well, I should think."

Three months before, he would have taken it from her for his own test, but now he leaned over her hands, examining what she held. She was better suited to the work than Calloway, and though he was always her preferred reanimator, Anne knew herself to be the superior Neurological Ingenieur. However, she had never attempted to remake a spine, as this German Ingenieur had done a few miles from where they stood. Platinum made sense: a superior conductor that wouldn't sicken them with verdigris, but expensive for a creature that only lived a week. Difficult to recover in the field.

She stood up from the table on which the creature lay, her hands still slick with blood and aethereal fluids. "I've never seen an automaton so complex."

"Is it really so different than ours?"

She stared at him. "They've successfully fused two bodies, Dr. Calloway, father attempted it at the end, but never succeeded."

"Well, certainly—"

"—and it's older," she said, irritated that he couldn't see what was in front of him. "Look. There—the seam is healing." The first sign of granulation along the lips of the wound, where two bodies had begun to fuse, bound together by more than just stitches and sparks, but by new scar tissue and the fine hyphae of the *Armillaria lazarites* which crossed the gap between skin and skin. A few miles from this spot, a cadre of German neurologists had created something alive out of patchwork. But she couldn't yet grasp their innovation, what exactly had allowed two nervous systems to expand and entwine, fusing seamlessly into this new sort of creature. The automaton's size—approaching twice that of an average man—was only possible if the nervous system had been enhanced to control the additional flesh. Otherwise, it would be like those creatures she had seen in London laboratories: a single man's nervous system trapped in the grafted flesh of other bodies, collapsing under limbs with which it had no communion.

When Calloway returned to the basement where he reanimated Anne's automata, she sketched what she could grasp of the automaton's experimental physiology, identifying the various bodies from which it was composed, the layering of muscle and the elaborate network of wire that united its elements.

IN FRANCE, sleep often came in fragments, like shrapnel, full of vertigo and disorientation. Dreams often drove her back to work, padding night-gowned to the basement rooms where the bodies lay. But perhaps that, too, was a dream because rather than the unnamed corpse below her hands, she felt the drag of catgut through father's skin, and then the needles she pressed into his fingers every day for a year, to track the nerve's regeneration. The first ichor she ever saw dripped from her father's forearm. She had been sixteen: his nurse and secretary and amanuensis.

"There," he said, dabbing the fluid, "look Anne. This runs from your brain through every nerve in your body. This is life itself, the fluid that makes us what we are."

On Sunday afternoons, his left arm in a sling, he sketched diagrams on the dining room table and quizzed her with Gray's *Anatomy*. She saw the most intimate workings of life laid bare in his theatre: cadavers, crying dogs, a monkey. He had showed her the internal workings of his own arm. He described the Vagus nerve, the body's largest, and its suitability for wired automata. Father had called it the wanderer, that binds brain to heart to gut, the nerve of dropped guts and the clutch of heartbreak. He told her, "When you fall in love, my dear, it will be the Vagus nerve that knows first. So it was with your mother. My stomach fell and I could not breathe when I saw her the first time." Had her stomach fallen and her knees weakened the first time she kissed John? She could not remember. She had felt that with Violet from the moment of her birth.

The night she examined the Giant, bad dreams once again drove her from her bed. She lit the lamp, then pulled out her sketches of the Giant. She imagined peeling back its skin, opening a long channel down its spine to explore the muscles grafted to its shoulders, to count the seams and follow the hair-thin platinum wires to their intersections, mapping the fused flesh and discovering not two bodies, but at least four.

Shortly before dawn she began her report, describing the automaton's magnificence and complexity, but she worried the War Office might find her reverence unpatriotic so she struck out those sentences and began again. She wished her father could have seen it. She wished she could have seen it walk. The legs had been elongated with metal armatures, supported by secondary and tertiary layers of muscle fit to the sartorius. They had accomplished something magnificent.

3

NED

Like most boys, Ned knew automata in stories from his grandparents, and then in penny dreadfuls, where they were a staple threat to pretty blonde heroines. The magazines were luridly illustrated with the risen bodies of the dead, who were shambling and well-muscled, staggering through gothic cathedrals and battlefields while pretty women fled in white gowns. No one had seen a real automaton in years, as far as he knew. Boys might play at them, with one a knight, and the other a monster. Or you might imagine a small war in some foreign jungle or desert, where ragged bands of colonial automata fell before the gatlings in your infantry square. But automata themselves were archaic, belonging to earlier sorts of warfare, or foreign places, falling before the far more effective thin red line. When he hid such a magazine in his desk, and his schoolmaster found it, the class received a lecture on their uselessness. They live no more than a week at the outside; they are too short-lived and too clumsy for complex instructions. A good one might chop wood or carry water, but don't expect them to work in a factory, nor operate a rifle. King Arthur had his automata, perhaps, but not Frederick the Great, nor Napoleon. The North West Rebellion in Saskatchewan had its automata, and where are the Métis now?

He'd read a story about someone raising the dead in a faraway place. Alabama. Haiti. It began with a moment of horror, sudden death, and a hysterical mother, a grief-maddened grandfather used antique ceremonies to raise their beloved dead for a few more hours of life. If one could call the shambling body alive. Those creatures were curiosities, peculiar natural phenomena with little utility, remnants of a far stranger and more terrible world.

Despite that early education in their irrelevance, Ned found he had a knack for finding them in France: a silhouette in the moonlight; the way a long arm lay crooked on the earth; the bright wire that hung from a skull. He filled his pockets with the bright filaments, wondered about the metal's origins: donated rings and necklaces and watch chains from Berlin, he imagined, remade into monsters.

This one was sunk in the October mud, an open gash in the throat, brain exposed.

Then he saw its four eyes across two skulls on a single neck. He had thought he was beyond shock after two years in France, but he cried out when he realized what he saw, then called l'Esperance over, and together they had rolled the body onto the stretcher. One hand of its five opened and closed and opened. One spindly arm had survived the mortar blast, but the other two torn off at the elbow were thicker than tree stumps. What he had pushed onto the stretcher—against l'Esperance's protests that the man was worse than dead—had been a series of lumps, heavily scarred under the misshapen sack of a uniform. He had never seen scarring like that, not even on the Potsdam Giant.

"Another one?" the Sergeant said when they returned to the advance dressing station. "Well, Calloway's got latitude no man should ever possess. It's bad for the soul to do that kind of work. He has no idea what he asks."

"I can't—"

"—if you're one of Calloway's you'll have to go with the beast. Lord knows why."

By then l'Esperance had disappeared, leaving him to the unfriendly company of the dressing station. Another hour beside the stinking, shuddering body, stranger and stranger in the twilight of the fires, with the real work he ought to be doing far behind him. Waiting, he helped one man—half his face in bandages—toward the wagon that would take him elsewhere. He helped a nurse with basin after basin of bloody cotton.

The body still shuddered when, long after dark, the Sergeant tapped him on the shoulder. "They've come," he said, "to take you to Calloway. Better go. They don't like to wait."

A large cart loaded with bodies. The two orderlies —heavy men with dull eyes—moved steadily and without haste.

"Hello," Ned said, "I have something for Dr. Calloway."

"You'd better come along, then," said one of them. "This here?" and together the three of them dragged the Giant onto the heap of bodies.

"How far is it?" he asked.

"Not far."

"I have to be back, you see."

"Yes."

"I have duties. I'm not Calloway's man."

"No."

In the back of the cart he heard something shudder. For the first time the two orderlies started, looking back. "It's not dead?" one asked. The other muttered, "I thought it was dead."

"It's been doing that. He's dead, I'm sure of it."

"They're all dead," said the second orderly, "but dead doesn't always mean what it used to."

They arrived sometime after midnight but before dawn. He wound the thin filament of platinum around his ring finger and thought, if I had a girl, I could give her this, and imagined marrying in a white church somewhere, the ring washed clean. Then he ignored the fancy, and unwound the filament.

Behind him, the automaton's left hand continued its twitch, now close enough to the edge of the cart to make a sound. *Tap. Tap. Tap.* Despite the absence of half a skull and the tangled wire that dragged in the mud and wound around Ned's wrist, the hand still tapped.

In the cold room on the main floor Ned was alone with the automaton and the tapping grew louder. He knew the sound was the trick of silence, but it was impossible to ignore. *Tap tap tap.* As though the automaton's limbs still tried to communicate some last message through those spasmodic fingers. *Tap tap tap.* Not morse code.

He twisted the arm so the fingers faced upward. Now they tapped the air. This close to the body its scent was staggering: stale blood, ruptured intestines, mud. In the airless room, he could smell something else, too, sharp and metallic, like the air before a lightning storm, or the smell of a machine shop. Then— this was peculiar, a trick of the room—a sound, like a voice.

"Nine," it said. "Nine."

He jumped back. He'd been assured they couldn't speak, and no trace of human sentiment remained.

Then Anne was beside him, her hair covered, but

shedding filaments finer than the platinum still wrapped around his wrist.

"He's talking," he said.

"They can't. They're in pieces—"

"Listen."

"Nein."

She crouched at his head, listening to first one mouth, then the other until she felt the faint vibration from the central throat. She touched its shoulder, where exposed filaments still shone.

"Is this all you found?"

"I think so. How can he speak when he's missing his skull? Even if he has two?"

"Have you ever killed a spider and seen it twitch?"

"Nein."

"It's not life as you or I live it. It's not pain or thought as we know it. It's a different order of existence. Where did you find it?"

"A trench. The Australians took it."

"Nein."

Softer now, as though the automaton was falling asleep. She knelt beside it and with a gentleness that horrified him, touched the cracked bone of its skull. Then a flicker of her skirt and she was gone. He waited—mouth full of questions, wondering if she'd return—then took his courage in his hands and followed after, her steps faint on the stairs, then down a hallway, through a door where she was waiting for him in a room papered with diagrams.

"Miss Markham? Do you—" Here he offered her the wire, ring-shaped and warm from his skin. She reached out for it, and without thinking he slipped it on her finger, a funny little ceremony that had come upon him unplanned, but revealed the truth: he had wanted her since that glimpse weeks before, the girl at the end of the corridor in the white overall, her sleeves stained to rust-colour.

"I want to know more," he said. "Tell me about them."

"You brought me the Giant, didn't you? That was the first I saw of the really new kind. Thank you for that." Her smile transformative. He blushed.

They sat together in what had been a handsome drawing room, green paneling and gold brocade moved aside to make room for large tables and typewriters. She showed him the diagrams. This one might fly, though not until we know more about how to hollow bones and merge avian air sacks with human lungs. This one crouches low behind the walls of ruined cities, made for reconnaissance. This one can carry a crew of five, firing mortars across no-man's-land, directed by the officers who whispered commands into various brains. This one is infinitely extendable, flexible, made of as many bodies as one can find. More than that. A dozen bodies. Twenty.

"But I don't know enough. Not yet. I'm learning, though, every day."

When she spoke about giants her face was bright,

almost pretty. Her scalp a stubble of blonde-grey hair, but nevertheless like a little girl showing off her picture cards. His littlest sister had smiled like that when she drew tippy horses on the back of an envelope and said *look here Ned! Look!*

"They keep telling me no, you can't waste time in experimentation, which means we're stuck the same over and over. You can see that the Germans have improved on the old automata. You've seen them." She picked at the skin of her knuckles with a finger bloodstained by the prick of her needle. "What else have you seen? From the Seventeenth army? You were at Valenciennes? I have guessed they had a centre at Valenciennes."

She watched him with those peculiarly pale eyes, silver-white, and he thought of what he had seen in the darkness, indistinct burrowing creatures that tore through minefields, or marching giants. When soldiers saw them rising up out of the trenches like monsters or myrmidons, they all went cold inside, the shock freezing all their training from their bodies, until the only thing that kept them facing forward was the knowledge that some NCO had a gun pointed at their backs. And you might know that behind you or down the front to the south, there were similar creatures fighting for your side, for what was good and noble. But such a thing was hard to believe when the vision of them emerging in the mist of dawn or the dust of artillery fire was so dreadful.

4

ANNE

Early in October, Beauchamp summoned her to speak with an Austrian Neurological Ingenieur captured after an attack near Thiepval, during a period that would later be called "The Battle of the Somme," though all Anne knew was the influx of bodies and the distant noise. The Austrian had been outside the village requisitioning the freshly dead while under fire, until the redoubt fell. Unusually for Ingenieurs in combat, he had survived long enough to be taken prisoner.

She had no way of knowing who he was until she saw him.

"Herr Doktor Schellenberg," she said.

Schellenberg looked up through the surviving lens of his glasses and licked at the blood on his lip.

"Bärchen," he said.

He was older than her father, she had thought as a

little girl, but not yet a grandpapa. He often brought her chocolates from Vienna, and once a little bear from Berlin he had wound up and set stalking clumsily across the breakfast table. He had said, "schöne Bärchen!" and she had answered "Rawr!" Bärchen stole sugar from the bowl under his direction and nibbled her toast. He had visited several times a year then, and sent Christmas cards with tinsel, which she always saved from the January fires. When she was fourteen, she had assisted him in one of her father's surgeries. The visits had stopped for some reason father would not explain, though she gleaned some of their disagreement regarding automata and the possibility of conscious resurrection for the newly dead.

"I have belief you are safe here," she answered, slipping into rusty German. Captain Beauchamp glanced over at her, as though surprised. "Would you like something to drink? I have none of coffee. And tea. But there is water."

He nodded.

"It is living rough here. You have better organized lab I am believe. I have always hear that your trenches are well maintained." Her German was clumsy with disuse, frustrating.

"Bärchen," he began.

"—Anne, sir. I have not been Bärchen for years now."

"Your father. I was sorry to hear it. His last investigation was too much. He should not have attempted the sciatic."

"Combined with his sleepiness. Exhaustion. I think, yes, it was too much. He worked in the hospital until the end, and the time did not have to recover."

"The world is an uglier place without him. I had thought, when this was all over, we would compare our work. I had thought I would come back to the little house in Surrey and we would drink tea together on the lawn."

A moment of silence. Somewhere, far away, she heard the orderlies drag bodies over rough floors. They should be more careful with such delicate mechanisms. The squeal, somewhere, of pigs.

"You have I think I believe expanded on some of his research. I see your work."

"Oh? I am surprised to hear it, Bärchen."

She didn't correct him that time.

"The beast. Giant." She groped after the words in German, but all she could remember was the Greek, "automaton. Two bodies together in one."

"Yes. We have made great strides. Your father's research—"

Here Dr. Schellenberg stopped. He looked at Beauchamp, who appraised the Austrian with bright, brown eyes.

"But I am not safe here. I'm not safe."

She glanced over at Beauchamp, who spoke in

German more awkward even than her own, "You could be made to be safety."

Dr. Schellenberg turned his attention to the officer, and they seemed to appraise one another. Irritated, she said, "can we at least get him away from the line?"

"You're not in a position to make promises, Miss Markham, but if Doctor Schellenberg could tell us a little about the Giant, we would consider it a gesture of good will."

Dr. Schellenberg waved his hands and said, "I understand."

"Then, Miss Markham, what would you like to know?" Captain Beauchamp asked.

"Can you tell me what alloy you've used?"

"Platinum. Iridium. Gold, for its capacitance and how well the flesh tolerates it. But wire is only necessary for the initial revivification. We have tried extracting the metal from automata once awoken, though that is risky. Now we leave it to recover later."

"Do you use father's strain?"

"No. It is a new strain, seeded into the body as near to life as one can, or as your father did, in life. The greatest innovation, though—" Dr. Schellenberg hesitated. "The—we call it ichor—must be alive, for want of a better word. You have a brief window between the death of the body and the death of the ichor. Seconds. Perhaps a minute if there is no fever. It is better to draw it from a living body into the dead in the moment one electrifies it."

Blutwasser? Ichor. Blood of the gods, but also the weeping fluids of an ulcerated wound. That might be English, though, Or French? *Sang des dieux*.

"What my father called Animal Electrical Fluid."

Schellenberg nodded. "Yes, yes. That is the substance. It is—this your father never understood, I think, though given time I think he would have discovered it—alive in a way unlike our bodies. It is—life itself, perhaps that is too dramatic. But the substance is. Like the alchemist's quintessence, a kind of infectious agent, but in the right circumstance, with the application of current, the presence of your well-developed hyphae of the automaton, and the network of precious metals, the infection is animation."

"Furthermore," Anne said, and thought again. *Indessen*? "But, the faradaic current—"

"—the ichor must be alive. That is the reason your father's work on the ulnar nerve was so successful, and why he could control the frog's leg when he used gold wire and his own arm. It is not the faradaic current alone, though that is what his papers suggest —it is his own living ichor that brought about this great success. This alloy is superior to your copper, more sensitive, and in combination with the living ichor, it animates the deserted flesh, so long as it is colonized by our strain of lazarites. Now we can build living creatures out of many bodies. You have seen it yourself." His voice rose here, exultant.

As he spoke, she sketched. He watched, correcting this term, or that. "No, the Vagus nerve is superior—it makes a better bond with the lazarites. Yes, you may run the wire along the skin, or just beneath it, but the process is clumsier. Better to use that architecture already in place."

"We found an automaton at Thiepval." She began in German but gave up and continued in English. "It was made of at least two men, perhaps more, and the bodies had begun to grow together at the seams—I have never seen automata that can heal, nor one that can choose to walk across no-man's-land. I could not tell in my dissection—the rot was too far advanced— but did you destroy the cingulate cortex?"

Dr. Schellenberg shook his head. "This is the next innovation, after the platinum and the living ichor. The cingulate cortex must be directly inoculated, which destroys it in part, but not entirely. Else you have nothing but a machine, an inefficient and shoddy locomotive, fitting for the defence of Prague, or Thermopylae—but unsuitable for the Deutsches Heer."

"But—their consciousness persists? Past the initial revivification?" She felt a strange clutch in her heart as she began to understand the automaton she had so recently examined, brought from Thiepval by a young Canadian pressed into service by Beauchamp.

"Perhaps. I have never clearly established one way or the other. But I believe it is the living ichor and the hyphae that produce a different sort of automaton. The work is troublesome, though, and unreliable. It requires a delicate hand—like yours." He reached across the table toward her fingers, which rested on the page of her sketchbook.

The man from the War Office leaned forward. Schellenberg withdrew again. "Bärchen," he said, "it is good to see you. I think. I think I have seen your work, too, fine stitches along the spine, no?"

"Herringbone is strong. It lies flat."

"We are not so particular about the stitch."

"No." She agreed and thought of the magnificent creature she had just seen, its height and power, the clumsiness of their execution, one leg dragging behind the others, its metal armature jutting through the remaining skin of its back.

Without looking, she drew a violet on the top right-hand corner of her page, then added a frame around her diagram, shy leaves and buds tumbling down the curve. She drew a trench across her notes, the zigzags, the redoubts, the support lines. One question remained. She was afraid of the answer.

"Do you know why it ran into no-man's-land?"

Schellenberg seemed to think, and she remembered those long Sunday afternoons in summer, her father and his guests talking through their work. Its possibilities. Its risks. He was still that man, then, not so damaged by two years of war that he could not think like a scientist. "I think perhaps our methods allow for greater awareness than the automata of the past. I think, perhaps, a kind of memory persists."

She nodded, and thought of how her own automata felt on waking, when often she touched their cool flesh and led them by the hand from the laboratory. Calloway found her attention to them distasteful, a strange kind of intimacy with the dead that made no sense to him, who had always thought of them as he thought of anatomy cadavers or the inert bodies of anaesthetized dogs. Not men any longer. Perhaps clay.

"I have seen what you do with copper—those webs are effective until the metal corrupts, and verdigris kills them as it kills us. Anne. Anne. Your materials are antique. The world is wider now, and—oh!—the things we will accomplish—"

Another glance at Captain Beauchamp.

"When this is over I will write a book. We will collect what we have learned, all us poor scientists divided by madness. We are cosmopolitans. We are no patriots. What automata we might make together if you understood our work, and we had your skill."

"Talosites," she said.

"That was your father's term."

"No," she said, surprised to hear herself speak the truth, remembering the drawings she had seen of Talos circling Crete, a vein of fire running through his thigh, the molten ichor of the gods under his bronze skin. The substance of life itself. It had seemed natural: Talosite, she had said to Father, look at how well it suits. He had agreed. It had shown up in his next monograph. "Mine. It was my name from the beginning."

5

NED

They had a little ritual when he brought an automaton to the villa. He came to find her, under the guise of a report, and they sat together, him telling the story of its capture, its peculiarities, and her listening, marking up her naps, sketching without thinking as he described the figure in action. She asked questions; he clarified. The first time they met this way it was almost an accident, when heavy rain delayed his return to his unit, and they sat up near the fire, waiting for transport, talking.

When he saw the creature in no-man's-land, he knew Anne would be enchanted. Like the first Potsdam Giant whose arrival had ushered him into this strange work, it was made of multiple bodies grafted, but this one was taller, limbs disproportionately long and spindly with metal armatures jutting out from under the skin. Anne glowed when she saw it, and after a quick examination of the articulated limbs, she told him it was important, a new innovation on the part of the Deutches Reich's Ingenieurs. It was in the cold room down below, where Récamier was at work dismantling them, Ned knew, so Anne could examine the workings. Anne had cross examined him in what had once been a parlour, huddled near the fire, asking him how it had walked before the machine guns took it down, why it was out in daylight, how long it had lain in the mud before he could collect it? Had it spoken? Well, then, what had it said?

He stood close to the fire, shivering with his great coat drying on the back of a chair. She asked her questions—what colour was its skin? Did it struggle? Did it bleed?—and boiled water in an old kettle.

"There isn't anything in the kitchen? I could go—"

"—No, it's dreadful down there. It's the steppes of Russia. And shut up for the night. This will have to do." Then a basin, steaming in the chilly room, so he could wash. The luxury of lady's soap and a nearly clean towel, which she brought uneasily, as though she did not want to wait on him, but saw no alternative.

"Thank you, ma'am," he said. "It's real nice to have a wash." He sounded so colonial when he said it. "Real pleasant," he repeated. Then, "pleasant." Then he was silent, and she looked at him, her pale, prominent eyes appraising him with an unfeminine directness.

"I'm going to make tea. Would you like some?"

Giving up on speech, he nodded. The mug was heavy and white, not very clean. Together they drank tea bitterly strong and hot, and for a few minutes their fingertips were warm. Or maybe hers were always warm. His were always freezing.

A minute of silence he did not know how to break. Then she said, "Ned, have you noticed anything new?" He must have looked bewildered. "Among them," she clarified.

"The giants?"

"The automata. Have they changed since you first saw that giant?"

He thought. "They're larger," he said.

"And?"

"Bigger."

Those pale eyes narrowed. She dug under her scarf to scratch her scalp, and as she did a green-gold hair came away in her hand, caught in the firelight.

"They smell different. Like different kinds of rot."

"Oh!" she said, suddenly alert, a hunting cat. "There it is. Like what?"

"Like earth. Like digging in the garden. And I saw one that must have been twelve feet tall. I only just saw an outline in the moonlight, walking along the supply trench, out of range. You couldn't see an ordinary man, or a horse, but you could see it."

It had been like a distant giant out of fairy tales, he had wanted to write Franky and say, what do you think of this, then? But Franky was gone. He continued to observe, as he had been taught to do by Captain Beauchamp, not to plan an assault, but to detect the creatures of nightmare.

"I think," he said.

She waited, her face so still she might be a picture.

"It had more than one head. A bunch of heads. A ... cluster."

She breathed deeply.

"How many arms?"

"I couldn't see it. It was moonlight. I don't know what I saw, not really."

"I do. I know."

She produced a letter, German, written in a vigorous, tangled hand. She flipped pages and showed him a diagram, a creature with four heads joined at the neck, arms running down either side of the body. Four legs. In one diagram it stood upright, in the other it rolled forward, balancing on all ten limbs.

"This?" she said. "Is it this?"

"No."

She deflated.

"It was larger."

"Oh!" she said. "They've done it, then."

She did not speak for another moment, but without looking reached for a large sketchbook. From it slipped a silver pencil, elaborately worked with vines and flowers, polished where her fingers held it. She flipped to a new page and began drawing what he had described. When she finished she said, "Next time get closer. I want to know what they've accomplished. It's remarkable work. Remarkable. All of it is happening just across the line. If I had been there—"

He saw the other diagrams on the page: a creature with hooves and a human head; a man-shaped body made of wolves.

"Are those other German giants?" he asked.

"Oh no. These are mine."

And then she began to speak, turning the pages so Ned could see her real ambitions. She sketched as she spoke, her hands seeming to work of their own accord, as his mother's hands did when she knit on winter nights. Her sketchbook was full of flowers—violets—and monsters made of many men. Animals, too, he now saw, emerging under her fingers as she spoke with him, while in the basement—he knew—Récamier dismantled his most recent acquisition, an automaton made of at least four men, possibly five. He tried not to think of that, focusing instead on the barest, faintest curve of a smile on her lips as she described her jumbled plans, her dreams, her ambitions to make creatures beautiful and useful, to recover the dead into Talosites that towered above them all, like the Israelite's angels, wings and flaming swords and burning glances from a thousand eyes.

But then, as though she knew the strangeness of

what she described, she covered the page with her hand, closed the book. What she did next shocked him more than anything else he had seen in the last twelve hours. She kissed him. And her mouth was small and hot with tea.

Later, he was lying on the floor and she was astride him and it seemed her eyes weren't a pale blue, but white. Staring at the opposite wall, unseeing, her scarf fallen from her head, and her short greenish hair a spider-web nimbus around her head. He had never—not in all his life—seen a being like her. He was not entirely sure she was a woman, but another kind of creature, also from ancient stories: the sidhe, the tylwyth teg.

Down her left inner arm ran a long, well-healed scar. He kissed its length, then kissed its intersections, where other scars crossed it, and then kissed the white points of sutures.

6

ANNE

Not long after Anne's interview with Herr Doktor Schellenberg, Beauchamp sent word that they'd taken his laboratory during the night's advance. It was an operation so quick, so pointed, the Reich's Neurologisch Ingenieur Korps couldn't evacuate, nor destroy the equipment, the benefit of intelligence gained from Schellenberg's further interrogation.

Like the German trenches, Schellenberg's laboratory was a substantial organization, nothing like the temporary quarters Anne knew. There was a morgue, two operating theatres, a ward for the dying. Anne followed Beauchamp through the double doors to the entrance, where two men waited. One was an orderly, she guessed, the other an Ingenieur, and she nodded to him, wondering if she had known him as a child, or read his name in one of father's letters.

In the ward, there were half a dozen narrow metal beds on which bodies were mounded under blankets, or so she thought on entering the room. In fact each body was thickly matted with lazarites.

Calloway pulled her back from the door.

"What is it?" she asked.

"Contamination." He said sharply, as though she was a subaltern who ought to know better.

She laughed.

"Don't be silly, Calloway. We're inoculated a thousand times over. Though I would prefer Father's strain to whatever they've been using here."

She turned again toward the dead, those draped silhouettes that had once been people, and now sprouted fruiting bodies that sent microscopic emissaries into the air in search of new hosts on which to wait for death and the inexorable march of fungal time. Father had spoken of the mycelial kingdoms which intersect so beautifully with the kingdoms of the human brain, whose branchings echo the deltas that running water will cut in earth, or the divisions of a root. We are all built with the same structures, he told her, what possibilities are there for unity across species and material?

"They must have been alive when they were inoculated. It can't have spread so widely if they've only been dead a day or less."

Calloway made a strangled noise. "To what end, though? What were they doing—"

"They're doing just what we are a few miles west. But more efficiently."

Calloway said something else, then, perhaps how can you laugh, Anne? Or what would your father say, Anne? But she was already deep in the ward, noting that all the dead still wore blue-striped pajamas, that two were legless, and a third sprouted masses of white threads where his face had been.

She reached out a hand to touch it, watching the filaments collapse like dust motes or spider's webs beneath her fingers.

"It's the new strain Schellenberg described, that can begin populating a body while it is still alive, and then—"

But Calloway had retreated into the hallway.

The magnificent creatures Ned brought to her had their origins here, in the delicate white veil of the lazarites. In bodies converted to these purposes at the end of their human lives, rather than after their deaths. It hurt her, deeply and sharply, to know that these men had been interrupted in the middle of their transformation, and had not reached their well-earned place in some huge and multifarious creatures that should stalk the hillside on a hundred legs, shot through with platinum and ichor and the pale, searching filaments.

"Damn them all," she said under her breath, then she could not stop the words from growing louder in her mouth: "Damn them. Damn them."

Behind her, footsteps, but who cared that someone was listening? She walked down the ward toward the nurse's station, then through to surgery, where some procedure had been interrupted, leaving behind bloody cotton in white enamel bowls. Through there to the still rooms, no longer mechanically cooled and suffused with the scent of rot and old blood. A Schellenberg Automaton attached to the green glass batteries. Its ichor too far gone to revive.

She regretted that second death and imagined instead what its first moments of consciousness should have been: Schellenberg presiding over the glass batteries, the smell of electricity and ozone, then a blue flame rippling through its body, the unifying, galvanizing flood of newness: platinum fusing to nerve fusing to hyphae, as the new composite creature lurched into consciousness in a body that did not entirely belong to it. A strange kind of birth, transformative and violent.

Calloway had rejoined her. He wore a mask. "Anything useful?"

"So many things," she said. "So very many!"

"But what do you wish to take?"

She hesitated over the birth room. The theatre of assembly, as Calloway called it.

"All of it," she said. She walked away, aware that what she asked was ridiculous, that she should be selective, and require less of the orderlies, and of Calloway, but she also felt a rising defiance inside her, a desire to ignore what was reasonable, a recklessness, a disregard for the niceties taught by great aunts and required of fathers, or fiancées, or the straitened circumstances of wartime motherhood. Without those limits, why should she be reasonable? Why should she not find out what lay on the other side of unreason, of these long, unsleeping nights, and the plans she made for creatures more magnificent and stranger than anything nature invented.

She went to Schellenberg's office next and sat down at his desk, examining his surviving notes, observing that he had been a poor draftsman, but a diligent record keeper. Bodies coming in and bodies going out. A journal of ideas, uninspired, but evidence of their techniques and procedures. There was, she thought, none of the ambition she had seen in Schellenberg's eyes. No sense of what this could mean, in the right hands, of how far a body could be reshaped to serve other purposes.

Having taken the notes and the diagrams, Anne began to recognize Schellenberg's designs in the new Talosites that Ned brought her, further elaboration on the principles he had discussed in their brief meeting, innovations the Germans no doubt still undertook in other laboratories. They were growing more complex, she noted in reports to the War Office, though the War Office seemed to ignore her. When Ned brought her a seven-legged creeper, she could see where the automaton's other half had been torn away, German anastomosis clumsy but effective. She could do something far finer, more precise, allowing for a more carefully modulated interaction of parts, not simply the cruciform, eight-limbed Talosites she had tried and failed to build, but two bodies intertwined. Or three. Then four. Then a hundred.

The creeping, spider-walking creature with its three legs was part of something much larger, lost in the mud. The skull had been blown away. One head? Two?

That night in her sleep she saw the dead rising: John and little Violet, her father and mother and brother, Millicent and the other girls in the munitions factory. And more ancient than those, the dead in variety and sympathy, entwined nerve to nerve and heart to heart, until they had made another sort of creature, a composite creature, multi-limbed and many-eyed. John's hand on Violet's blended, until she saw not her lover and their daughter but a new creature, singular, made of arms that twisted about arms, and nerves that rooted in other nerves. The beautiful intermingling of all the dead. A thousand limbs. A thousand eyes. A thousand hearts in one, making their way across the ground on borrowed legs and bloody stumps.

When she woke, she sketched it in her notebook, beside the diagrams for copper wire. She carried her notebook to the kitchen and drank tea before dawn, and when the cook came in to light the fires and brew bitter coffee, she had already determined the first creature of her new career.

Large. Radially symmetrical, made of limbs extending from a spinal core, creeping and rolling across the earth, multiple brain centres and eyes meant that there was no up, nor down, just the star-shape of the body and limbs specialized for neither grip nor locomotion, but capable of all tasks. Then she might have been asleep, because next she saw an eight-legged creature, horse and man, low-weighted to run heavy loads across rough ground, with the simple instructions her creations could conceive: follow this man from place to place. Something simple, like a stretcher-bearer at first. Something with places to put the wounded, too, at intersections of the limbs, or in extra sets of limbs that worked in unison, like crab's legs, along the back. Calloway told her these dreams were impossible, though her notebook still filled with them.

Schellenberg would understand, but while she wrote him weekly, his responses were sporadic and the pages thumbed by any number of War Office Beauchamps. He rarely answered her questions directly.

I do not think you grasp the difference, he wrote in German, that living human fluid makes. While you may rely on horses and pigs, or even the newly dead, such materials will make short-lived automata that die in exhaustion and confusion after a week or two of unceasing activity. There is only one way to create a long-lived creature: decant living, human ichor directly into the automaton. You may cultivate the strains of lazarites your father selected, and build the elaborate creatures you have imagined, but until you have found a way to feed their bodies living ichor, your automata will die as children. Do you want them to speak to you, Bärchen? Do you want to hear what they would tell you? Then you must find a way to awaken them wholly.

When she had read the letter three times, she brought Calloway the problem of living ichor. He only said, "Hasn't it worked with the horses before? The spines are certainly compatible."

"But if what he says is true, it won't extend their lives much at all."

"And it's more suitable than the fluid of a corpse. By Schellenberg's argument, at least."

"You saw what they're doing on the other side. How can we possibly ignore their innovations? They're using civilians—"

"—no, Anne—"

"—it's obvious we must—"

Calloway turned on his heel, which was foolish moral indulgence. Why should the levée en masse ignore the dead when their vacated bodies might save the living? Military. Civilian. Animal. None of that mattered in the democracy of death, but materiel was Calloway's purview, with the help of two interchangeable young men from Edinburgh Medical School, who hardly spoke any more. And Récamier, of course. So until she visited the clearing stations and hospitals herself, she would have to accept his refusal.

She spun the platinum wire ring on her finger and returned to work, slitting the dural sheath of one body and stitching it to the second, then grafting muscle to muscle, then the fine tracery of platinum, and even as she worked on the new creature, she saw white dust overtaking the flesh, preparing it for the final transformation. And then, early the next morning, after a night spent stitching, it would go to Calloway, and the reinvigoration of the system with ichor from equine and porcine sources. And it would live for a few furious weeks, and then die its second death.

She could not help believe that there were better alternatives, and if the dying knew how precious their bodies were, they would not be so miserly as to keep them from use.

SHE WAITED until Calloway had gone to his room, worried he would look for her as he often did when, tired and drunk, he wanted to talk about St Bartholomew's, about the War Office's demands, about whether this would ever end. She worked rapidly, a little clumsily, collecting the minimum necessary components from Récamier's still rooms: a spinal cord and head with eyes intact, bathed in cold ichor from the horses. A single hand, palm up, attached by the loose ulnar, median, and radial nerves that ran from the wrist to the brainstem, linked with a nearly invisible four-strand cross stitch, a cruciate flexor that was not as tiny as she liked, but adequately bound the system together. She threaded hair-thin wire along the nerve-sheath, using tweezers and magnifying glass. Her hands were so cold by the time she had assembled a simple system—wire, green glass battery, spine—she had to warm them up before she could continue her work.

A cocaine solution injected just below the elbow for a regional nerve block. Then a tourniquet. In a minute her left hand felt like it was no longer hers, like meat attached to her body and she wondered if these were the sensations of a Talosite on awakening, a body both theirs and not-theirs, in parts alive with sensation, and in other parts still dead, moving in collaboration with minds they could only sense. An unhomely body. A stranger.

She held the ring for a moment, then made a neat incision in her left wrist and was surprised that in the silence she could hear her own flesh cut, its meaty resistance just like the tense muscle and cartilage of her Talosites, which resisted her needle in much the same way. Then the most delicate nick in the ulnar nerve's sheath, which should leave sensation in the thumb and forefinger intact, though damaged, and from which she should recover in a matter of months. Based on observation, she could most easily sacrifice the action of the smallest finger of her left hand. Then she stood over her derelict child, as drop after drop of that most precious, most dynamic materiel fell into the open spinal column on the white table before her. It would be an entirely new creature, one she had only ever imagined. A brainstem and a hand. A head with an eye. She activated the battery. The familiar snap and sizzle. A flash of light.

"What have you done?" The voice first, then Calloway's hand around her forearm. She couldn't feel it properly, just pressure on the thick, senseless flesh. Not hers, not Anne. Someone else's hand.

"I avoided the vein," she said, irritated. "I needed a living human sample."

"For what?" His fingers still tight on her wrist, her hand limp, whether from damage or cocaine or his grip, she could not tell.

On the white enamel table, the creature worked its jaw. The eye opened and rolled upward, appraising them with an intelligence she had never seen in a Talosite.

Its single hand flicked one finger, then two. The jaw again, working, working, but despite the movements of the tongue, no words, no oxygen drawn into lungs that no longer existed, but nevertheless wonderfully *alive*, invigorated by her own donated substance. But in so much confusion. She should have found a complete body to resuscitate, so that at least these moments would have been familiar. The eyes searched the room and stopped at her own. She said, "I am your mother."

Calloway broke the circuit.

"No!" she said, "don't! You'll hurt it!" But too late, the eyes ceased their searching.

PART II

SUMMER AND
AUTUMN 1918

1

ANNE

Her youngest and most intricate child lay on five straw mattresses she had commandeered for its bed. It had been reanimated the previous night by Calloway, under Anne's supervision. Today, she admired the heavily corded muscles she had assembled in its back, the skin split and expanded with inserts, like gussets, from other bodies: a horse, three French civilians who died in a fever hospital two days before, all stitched together with a double herringbone.

The Talosite shifted. The mattresses weren't enough, and she worried about it at night, despite the blankets she had also collected to warm its trunk and lower limbs. She considered that her next child would be furry, with a thick mantle of fat about its many shoulders, and around its core, to protect it through the winter.

"Can you hear me?" she asked, this time speaking toward the Talosite's clustered heads, where she had left intact the auditory nerve of one core body, enhanced with material from horses and dogs. She found the structure's simplicity appealing, an elaborate, many-limbed creature built around a single neurological and aesthetic core.

She had experimented with fusing the skulls of multiple human corpses, but with little success, and instead created a cluster of skulls, as of grapes or the eyes of insects, with the various brainstems and spinal cords intertwining lower down, where she had attached its limbs. As she worked, she had imagined a creature of many eyes like Argus Panoptes, both useful and beautiful. If its mouths could speak a human language she could ask it how it felt to see in a million directions at once.

"Hello," she said again. "My name is Anne. I am your maker."

The creature raised one arm. Then another. Another and another. The only sounds it made were the long exhalations of many mouths.

"I am your mother. I said maker before, which is also true. But I am mostly your mother. You don't have a father, not properly speaking, but you have a mother."

The creature turned, and five of its eyes appraised her. She pushed a basin of water toward it.

"You should drink."

It bowed one of its heads, and as that head dropped the other one did as well, their intersecting spines requiring that one portion of the Talosite follow the other portion's lead. Even now, when her practical knowledge had grown extensive with experiment and observation, she was not sure whether the cluster of brains conversed at all, or whether they negotiated by accident, feeling the tug from one side or the other without understanding the origins of the action, as though their body was not shared, but hijacked by some other entity. Like being possessed, she sometimes thought, like carrying a passenger, a little stranger, and finding one's body directed by its unknown, unseen commands.

With her good right hand, she filled a tin cup at the basin and held it to one of the other mouths, on the head nearest her, which worked soundlessly as the first head drank. The crusted eyes turned toward her voice. "Water," she said, and tipped it onto the waiting tongue. On other heads, other mouths opened in unison.

SOMETIMES SHE FELL asleep on the straw mattress beside her new creatures. Sometimes she dreamed.

For example: the summer she was twelve was brilliant, and on the day of father's public demonstration she wore a fussy pink silk dress that swished pleasantly about her legs when she walked. Her father had gone early in the morning, but she had waited until ten o'clock, though she was dressed before that, lounging in the entrance hall for her great aunt to finish dressing upstairs and descend in a fearsomely elaborate afternoon dress. She carried her prettiest pocket handkerchief, the one with the violets, so Anne knew it was an important occasion.

The lecture hall at the hospital was already full of people, close and hot and smelling strongly of young men and formaldehyde. Auntie didn't want to be there, but found a corner with the special students and the wives of several doctors, settled Anne down on a seat, and sat in silence and disapproval until one of the wives appeared, and Auntie could say, "Oh, Mrs. Cadwallader, such a pleasure! Do you think you could take little Anne under your wing for the duration? The heat—" As soon as Mrs. Cadwallader nodded, Auntie fled to the hall outside, and Anne did not see her until that evening, at home, when no word was spoken of what had transpired.

Her father gave his address; students scribbled notes. Anne knew some of what he described, from the drawings they did together on Saturday afternoons: this is the nervous system, this is the brain, this the spine, these the intersections of sensation and command.

Then he stopped. He stepped back and announced the real object of the meeting, and the room grew quiet in that rustling way, as though everyone held their breath and leaned forward in their seats, dropping their notebooks to the floor so they might not miss anything of what they saw.

He began by reminding them of stories everyone knew: the Jews in Prague, the Maori undead, the ancient stories of the Norsemen, where the bodies of dead warriors rose to fight again at the bidding of their jarl. That was all well known. But, father continued, at St Bartholomews they had so rationalized the process that it could be recreated, adapted, consistently applied, and improved. It was no longer the purview of shamans and priests, but could be the work of doctors as well.

Then Dr. Schellenberg led out a creature. It looked like a man, more or less. It wore clothes, which had been the subject of argument, she learned much later, her father arguing that a creature meant to be integrated into modern society ought to dress like it, and that the naked undead warriors of Thermopylae were irrelevant. It was sentimental to present him unclothed. These creatures would work in mines and factories when they were perfected, not storming about the countryside in breechclouts.

If she had been fastidious, she would have never seen her father, so occupied was he with his lab and his students. They carried her piggy back up the stairs to her father's lab, and chatted with her over the luncheon table on Saturday afternoons, talking shop and sketching plans on the chalkboard father kept in a corner of the dining room.

It ought to be familiar to her, this proto-Talosite. She should recognize the origins of her present work, and her innovations, when she remembered the airless morning at St Bartholomew's. She gasped when the creature reached them on stage, man-sized, but inhuman, dragging its left leg, its features grey with death, and its eyes searching the crowd. Had it sought out and found her eyes, as she often dreamed? She could no longer distinguish between her waking memories of the hot afternoon at St Bartholomew's and the dreams in which she revisited the hard wood benches and heard her father's voice in long discourse regarding the experimental use of metal reinforcement, the composite nature of the body they built. The ancients revived fallen warriors, yes, but never built bodies anew from steel and copper, from the bones of cattle and the skin of pigs. That was the brave new world Dr. Markham proposed, and which she, Anne, had ushered into being.

Did the Talosite—no, the automaton, because she had not yet named these siblings, her father's other children—cast its dead glance upon her and did she cry out toward it, as she had at the little dog in their garden, the open incision on its paw weeping aethereal fluids? Did she rise from her seat beside Mrs.

Cadwallader and run toward it? And when she reached it, did it fix her with those eyes, those infinitely deep and sad eyes, that nevertheless held a deep and superhuman understanding?

Perhaps. Or perhaps she sat in obedient stillness beside Mrs. Cadwallader and the other wives, smaller and smaller, drawn into their skirts and chatter, drawn into her own best dress, with the blue silk flounces at the hem. Perhaps it was only that night, in dreams, that she ran to this brother of hers, and pulled him toward the door, telling him to go away forever and ever. Then woke in the shrill screams of her nightmare, as the creature swivelled his heavy neck, and reached his cold hands toward her, as though she could help.

THE NEXT MORNING she was at work in her room, unaware that she had not slept until she heard birds singing in the pink-stained darkness. The clatter of a cart, and tired voices outside drew her away from her worktable to the window where, looking down into the murk of the courtyard, she saw the creature curled on its side in the cart, its many arms wrapped about its body. Then she saw the soldier who had brought it: Ned. Or Ned's shoulder, which was enough of him that she felt the pulse in her throat accelerate. She had kissed that shoulder the week before. She had hung from that shoulder, and felt its weight across her in sleep. The shoulder was covered in mud, attached to an arm that directed orderlies as they unloaded the cart together. It took five men. Récamier out in his shirtsleeves and braces, his hair uncombed, holding open the double doors to the still room. The Schellenberg Automaton and the five men descended the stone ramp to the basement, where the air was still and cool. The door closed.

Still outside, Ned paused as the darkness lifted, replaced by the pale gold of day. She thought, he will look up soon, and see me. She thought, I will kiss the sliver of skin that shows between his hairline and the top of his collar, the fragile skin often rubbed raw by wet wool. She thought, he will come in the house and climb the stairs and we will have breakfast together. We've never had breakfast together. She dropped the silver pencil she still held, unnoticed as she felt more pulse points: her throat and belly, her knees. Newly alert, unsettled, her heart accelerating as she thought, I don't want you to climb those stairs and startle me. But oh, I do, O Ned. Below her, he had ceased his contemplation of dawn and walked toward the doors to the foyer, where Calloway's batman (she had no batman) was probably carrying a tray with coffee and a newspaper. He'd be in the house in a moment. New pulse points: between her thighs, her lips. But now she recognized the sensations in her body, the sweaty palms and dropped stomach, the jitter in her step as she walked first to her dresser to comb her hair, then abandoned the project to dress, then abandoned that, and sat on her bed, hands folded in saintly patience and thought that soon, any minute, any second, from the noise of the main floor, the shout of voices, footsteps will resolve, he will slip past Calloway and Récamier, past orderlies and the batman, and he will find me. O Ned, find me.

It was different with Ned, the unexpected spark of pleasure, the genuine affection she felt for him when he slept, his grubby shoulder warm against her back in the narrow single bed. How she settled into his body as she had never done with John, who had remained alien to her, even when they were naked, his arms around her, his spunk gathering in a pool between her thighs. Around John, she had been enervated, prickly, full of tears that he attributed to his impending departure, which made him smile gently and kiss her. The tears, though, had not been for John precisely. Perhaps for the detonated world of her childhood, and the total unknowability of the man she said she loved, whose ring she had worn, and whose child she carried out of wedlock.

Because, really, she only knew John for three days, if you counted hours that mattered. The first had been New Year's Day 1915, while the world continued to end around them, father dead, and most of the house shut up because of the cost of fuel, and the great aunts wanting her to come stay with them in Shropshire. Perhaps to roll bandages. Arrange theatricals.

The aunts insisted on staying with her over Christmas, her first since father's death in November 1914. That visit was a special kind of hell as she tore through the house, donating everything she could to St Bartholomew's. Students and porters carried it away. She didn't recognize any of them, but all the men she'd known were in uniform, dead or enlisted, mentioned in dispatches, or quietly disposed of on the western front. Her aunts insisted she keep the orchids and the books on alchemy, the objets d'art from Egypt and Mexico, the ancient wooden cup that had been part of a mystery cult on Lesbos. The fragments of Pythagorean papyrus. His notes gone, including those she had neatly transcribed, and the manuscripts, which she had annotated for revision.

His final monograph for someone else to finish. Calloway wrote her from Paris, where he was at work forming the Ingenieurs, already developing wartime automata. She didn't open his letter until after Christmas.

She met John on New Year's Day during an afternoon call on one of her childhood friends, which she had undertaken at her aunt's insistence. He was twenty-five. On the first day they spoke for twenty minutes in Stella's drawing room. When she collected her coat in the foyer, he followed her, saying, "I'm going that way as well, Miss Markham." They dawdled in the rain, another forty-five minutes conversation with chilly noses and red fingers. She thought, as they reached the dark house that she now somehow owned, that she could kiss him if she so chose. She did not choose, but she liked to imagine it, his coat open and around them both, like a girl in an illustrated romance. She saw him a few days later, for another chilly walk, and that time she kissed him. She was sad to find it was no better than those earlier kisses she'd experienced with one or two of her father's students, clumsy and wet-lipped behind the camellias. This kiss was pleasant but indistinct, a kind of blank warmth. She had thought to be transformed by it. She was not.

By the end of January 1915, he was waiting for new orders, and she was no longer a virgin. By February she wore his grandmother's cameo ring and they were engaged. She did not yet know that she was pregnant, and there was Violet, just a drop of blood, a being becoming, the rough matter of creation not yet refined into chubby arms and eyes and a voice. By March, John was dead, but Anne was not, and Violet continued her progress from tadpole to human child. Anne found that the version of John in her mind seemed to be not him, but his photograph. She could not remember his middle name. Not the weight of his body, nor his kisses, nor the night they spent in Brighton, beyond the awkward and comic lies spoken at the front desk when they checked in to the dull little hotel. She remembered only the sepia of his portrait, which sat on her dressing table when he was alive, and then hid in her un-read bible. She thought she had loved him: she had certainly said it, and had wept when he died.

Anne had gone to live with the aunts, who were censorious, but let her have a little upstairs room, and had prepared convenient lies regarding her missing husband. Tell the truth, Anne had said, add a wedding ring if you must, but the rest can stand. He died at Neuve-Chapelle and he is Violet's father. We would have been married his next leave. It was ridiculous to care about the appearance of it, the particulars of a cake and a gown, when everyone in the world was dead or dying.

Violet had been startlingly beautiful, in a way that surprised the aunts, whose hearts melted the tiniest bit when she slithered out of Anne, brilliant and screaming. Their hearts might have entirely liquified if Violet had lived more than six weeks. Anne's whole world might be different, with a little girl toddling after her through the sunny rooms of a cottage. She would have bought a cottage with father's money. If Violet lived. If.

Millicent had said that after the first pain, widowhood was just emptiness, as though one's future has ceased to exist. Anne felt a kind of drone beneath her skin, which on bad days rose into a storm, a screaming. There were no words in this scream, just the fact of chaos and noise, as though it was not her mind that screamed, but her nervous system. On bad nights she padded barefoot and night-gowned down to her laboratory and found consolation in the meticulous work of stitching body to body.

2

NED

Later that morning they lay on the floor of her workroom, before her fire, the door locked and rain falling outside. In his arms, she startled from sleep as though from a dream of falling. As she often did on waking, she felt about her for her tools: a needle; a silver pencil. She told Ned about the latest Talosite now sleeping in the old stable before it was released to the War Office. "Did you ever see one?" she asked him, suddenly. "The wild kind, not one of ours. In Canada?"

"No," he fumbled, uncertain at first of what she asked. "Not before I came to France. But when my grandmother was a little girl on the farm, their neighbour had one to tear out stumps."

"Oh?" Here Anne sat up from where her head had been pillowed on the torn cushions of a chipped Louis Quatorze chair. "How long did it live?"

"Not long. Grandma was afraid of it, though she and her brothers used to watch it from the fence and dare each other to go near where it was working. She said it worked for a week, day and night, and then dropped dead on Sunday morning, while the farmer was at church. Or dropped dead again."

"What had it been? When it was alive the first time, I mean."

"I don't know. An Indian?"

"Do you know what strain they used?"

The question could only come from someone like Anne. "No," he said slowly, knowing she did not grasp the absurdity of her monomania. "Something from the old country, I suppose."

"They used to culture it on animal skin, feed it honey and blood until they needed it."

"Before your lot came along?"

"Before my lot came along they were all monsters. Some of them could take commands, as your grandmother told you. Now we have a wholly new sort of life. Or perhaps it's an afterlife."

She settled further into his arms, her brittle little chin digging into ribs until she relaxed, growing boneless and catlike, warm on his belly. Somewhere, far away, he could hear the orderlies at work on the bodies in the basement. He wondered if Calloway was fussing with his batteries. Perhaps one of her creatures now rose from the theatre of its creation. As his mind relaxed into a doze, the Talosite resolved behind his eyelids, he heard footsteps on the stair, a thin voice crying, mommy, mommy.

In sleep, he revisited his grandmother's account in its entirety, not the version he had told Anne, but the real story which he had only gleaned from whispers between the adults. The sound of the automaton's cries at night; the dog it had killed; the blackened blood of its death wounds, still staining its skin. When it dropped on that Sunday morning, they found it in pieces. This was the part of the story his grandmother did not like to tell—and no one knew who had done it, or whether the creature had destroyed itself in rage at its own second death.

"WELL." He heard the voice behind him. "Well. What is it? What is that. That. Thing." He turned and saw McGinty, young subaltern newly arrived from Canada, a few steps behind.

"It's a Talosite, Sir," Ned said. "It won't hurt you. Keep walking, Sir."

The young man fell back toward the line, while Ned knelt and examined the remains, trying to determine where they'd dig, where they'd cut. Anne would want it whole. Calloway wouldn't care, and he was more likely to be in the field.

"You know about this sort of thing, don't you—?"

"Wallace, Sir. And yessir. Calloway's people will sort it out."

"This is the first I've seen of them. Nothing like the diagrams in training ." He stared across the yard. "Can we look at them?"

"There's just one, sir—"

"—but it's ten feet long!"

"Yessir. It won't do you any harm. It's dying, though Anne says—" the name slipped out.

"Anne?"

"Miss Markham. She assists Calloway."

"A nurse, then? Or—Henry Markham's daughter? I'd heard about her as well. You've met her?"

"Yes."

"Is she pretty?"

There were new scars on her arms and legs now, precisely cut and carefully sutured with tiny, elaborate stitches. She was severe and pale and her eyes never seemed to focus on his face.

"No, sir," he said.

"That's unfortunate. I expect she's brilliant. Henry Markham was brilliant. My uncle follows the medical journals, so I know a great deal. We can go over and look?"

"You can, sir."

Ned waited another moment, but the man didn't stir from where he stood. He said, "Perhaps. In a moment. Someone will know at HQ. I'll put word through. They'll want to know what I found. Post haste." McGinty walked away, briefly looking back at the automaton.

Ned approached the Schellenberg Automaton. He was used to seeing them blown to pieces, but to see one complete, and in daylight, filled him with a startling emotion he could not name, something akin to sadness suffused with a dull, insistent anger. There was the spine of a man entwined around metal armature, vertebrae reinforced with steel, and the muscles growing into and over each other, threaded with white hyphae, branching. The body contained three heads, one atop the shoulders, and others further along, sprouting from the trunk. The head nearest him blinked. Blinked again.

He squatted beside it, near where its ear had been. He wondered why they had severed the ear.

"Hello." he said. "Hello."

There was a human limb nearby that terminated in the long, cutting claws of the badger. He touched it. It was cool, but under his fingers, it twitched. The skin abraded by digging, open cuts packed with clay.

"*Guten Tag*," he said.

The eye in the socket rolled.

"Bonjour."

The eye in the socket rolled.

"You. There. You. By the— You." The young officer had returned. In one shaking hand he held a small, gilt-edged notebook. "I've sent word about what I found. They'll be here—I don't know when. But soon, apparently. Apparently this is a significant find. There was someone from Calloway's party at HQ when I got through. They're quite excited. What did you call it?"

"A Schellenberg Automaton, sir. Our side calls them Talosites."

"Yes. I think I will write about this. What's your name? I'll mention you. A poem. I write poetry. But perhaps an essay. They'll want to hear at home—I have friends at the *Whig* who are keen to get more direct news from the front." At their feet, the Automaton twitched and Ned tried to find its limits, where its body ended and the mud began.

"I should meet Miss Markham, and include some observations of her father. Corporal—?"

"Wallace, sir.

Then the young officer was gone with his note-book, and Ned considered the last time he had seen Anne, her eyes still black and wide with the cocaine she'd taken to block the pain of her last incision. He wanted to ask her, why? What have you done? But too quickly, she answered his unasked question.

"It must be alive," she had said. "Calloway won't anymore, though some of the orderlies will let me. Would you volunteer?"

He took her left hand and kissed the angry red skin on its outer edge, below her little finger. He tasted the metallic salt of blood, as he always did, no matter how often she washed.

3

ANNE

Calloway joined her in what had been a drawing room, orders in hand. Thirty Talosites required for September, even after the twenty-four they produced for 1 August. They'd had two months for those. Surveillance giants, and creatures suited for carrying ordnance on long marches. Low-slung, she thought, many legs and heavily muscled articulations, like shoulders and hips, reinforced spines designed to carry loads through the night.

"How can they think—" he began. "Before September—" He sat heavily on the settee they'd drawn up to the table in place of dining chairs, which were smashed to kindling in a corner. She glanced over the memorandum.

It would have to be something entirely new, a plan she could sense, but not yet grasp. A body not unified by the spine on which it hung, but spread across many nervous systems, with sensations and commands running back and forth over networks, rather than travelling outward along a single line of command. If one part was destroyed, others would continue, finding new routes around shattered bones and blasted spines. Many limbs, so that, even in the case of a barrage, the whole might survive and carry on and find its constituent parts. Creatures who could be split in three by enemy fire and still carry out their duties. Creatures who could find their lost limbs and brainstems, carry them home to her and be reassembled in some new order. Creatures who, once released into the field, could find others like them, and merge, growing larger with each meeting, before dividing again at their platinum seams to scatter back into the world.

Calloway was resting his head on the table. She traced a figure in the empty air: gold lines intersecting, along the spine of a human man, spreading outward to take in other spines, from horses, she thought, to begin with. She had discovered the year before that her greatest mistake was anthropocentrism. A multi-limbed, multi-brained octopus.

"Octopus," she said, "More platinum."

"Anne."

"Spines intersecting, like a series of suns, or stars," she added. "Radial symmetry. I must be able to do it."

"What they want might as well be sorcery."

She waited a moment in case he wanted to expand

on the accusation of witchcraft, then went on, "A sea sponge. Schellenberg suggested a sea sponge. They're asymmetrical"

"I had heard he was in prison for the duration—"

"Yes, but it's in the War Office's interest to allow us some correspondence. He's still the best resource we have. Do you think the French will interfere when we send to the hospitals for more bodies?"

Calloway took the papers back, scanning for the passage she'd just read.

"Civilian bodies," she clarified.

She made a noise like one of father's snorts, "We've used the Scottish regiments, and the Prussians. The Australians at Hamel. Sepoys. Horses. I made Sleipnir."

She stood and the world spun to the left, as it often did in the mornings. Her eyes could not focus, and Calloway's face was a smudge between his neck and his hairline. For the last weeks he had seemed absent, though his body remained steadfastly obedient.

From that day forward, Calloway sent orders directly to her. In August they moved again, but she hardly noticed, so intent was she on dismantling an elaborate new Schellenberg Automaton that Ned brought her from a lab abandoned when Crown Prince Rupprecht of Bavaria retreated toward Mons. She hardly registered the change in atmosphere around her, until Calloway told her one night about

Amiens and the changing tides. The War Office, meanwhile, sent Beauchamp and his doppelgängers. Legions of Beauchamps, all with clipped moustaches and impeccably cut uniforms fastened with Phoenix buttons, each requiring a larger and more elaborate Talosite, suitable for the delivery of ordnance or surveillance at speed over newly gained trenches, and into the open ground of September's battlefields.

Anne received abandoned automata as Armeeoberkommando 17 made their retreat, and she travelled as close to the line as Captain Beauchamp allowed. She would have walked the frontline itself, to save those who died before she could find them. *The Kreuzshlüssel.* *The Tausendfüßler.* Schellenberg Automata designed after some memorandum from the office of von Hindenburg. The creatures were low and resilient, built so heavily that they could still function after being half blown away. A wriggle of limbs and eyes and loose platinum wire still struggled through the mud, retaking trenches. Anne saw der Dachs in early October, abandoned in a field, still buried where it had emerged with the sappers from a failed attempt to mine the Allied trench. Most of it remained hidden, shovel appendages and the claws of badgers set along the serpentine spines of fifteen bodies, interwoven so expertly they seemed to be one, twenty feet long, lined with limbs that terminated in entrenching tools. The powerful muscles of as many thighs and backs interlocking with the metal and claw to dig faster and deeper than any man could, short of a tunnel boring machine.

When they went to the field where it had been found after the advance, Calloway sank heavily to his knees and said, "What have they done?"

"Just what we've done. Perhaps you ought to leave this to me, Stephen," but he only leaned forward until his head rested on his wrists and knees, and she left him to the quiet for a few minutes, directing the orderlies—new ones she'd never seen before—to begin digging out der Dachs.

"How," Calloway asked, "do you know it's a, a— you called it—"

"Der Dachs? Consider that it was built to dig its way under the ground. And the claws."

"I hadn't seen the claws."

She reached down into the hole and touched the limb nearest her. The fingers worn away, but the muscle of the forearm twitching against her hand. Not warm, but quick, as though ichor's dynamism persisted independent of the will of the creature who had, once, possessed that limb, that worn-down hand, those bones. Who had once been warm, and perhaps held a girl's waist with it while they danced.

"Can't we leave it die?" His voice thick and mechanical. "Anne?"

She climbed down, following the bright glint of wire, saying, "If we let it die, they all died in vain. We'll bring it in."

The orderlies were watching for her command, their faces grey with exhaustion, uniforms muddy tatters from the day's work digging and carrying. The automaton was so much more efficient than they, built to dig, tireless. Perhaps also made to roll over the parapet and into an enemy emplacement, destroying the trench with its weight and the blades attached to its limbs. The entrenching tools were bound to the flesh with too-large stitches, full of mud, not integrated into the creature as they should be.

Then the ground beneath her heaved. She thought it was a shell until she realized that the creature had turned under the earth, knocking down one of the orderlies. Charles, she thought, or he might have been Richard. She struggled up in time to see one of the curled limbs unwind and smash the orderly's head like an eggshell.

Calloway made a sound like a prayer, or a cry, and knelt beside the body.

"Vial!" she said, maybe shouting. Calloway looked up at her, then down at the man and fumbled in his pocket for a glass vial. She made the incision at the orderly's throat, a tiny cut past the jugular. The vial warm in her hand, she tucked it into the bosom of her blouse to protect it, then climbed der Dachs to drip that precious ichor into one of its spines.

4

NED

He spent October in the mud, either chasing automata or waiting in camp, searching for firewood and hot water, playing cards and telling stories about the monsters they had all encountered: a hundred legs; a thousand heads. Around him stretcher bearers and doctors, medical units and company officers, runners and sergeants and telegraphers. Bivouacked against the cold, Ned found a canvas corner and waited for news, wondering if it was worth sleeping. He walked out past the latrines, west and south back the way they had come with their galloping liberation, toward the friendly villages, which would never be German again.

He walked ten minutes south and stopped at a farmyard zigged by a trench long since shelled and overrun, too decayed to tell who had dug it originally. He stopped on the parapet and wondered if he'd ever crouched opposite this position, been targeted from it, kept his head ducked in a long run with a body for Anne. Wondered if this had been the Other Side once, like the other side of death, or life. Heaven. Hell. One of those.

His eyes dry and sleepless, he was about to return to camp, and find out whether it was worth getting some shuteye when he saw the automaton, not its flesh, but a bright filament of wire down the collapsed wall of the trench. Without meaning to, his eye followed it, and then his feet, along the breastwork to a dugout, stove-in, bones showing in the mud, and the remains of a camp. A cup. A smashed handful of bullet casings. The wire. He thought he heard something, a groan, or a chatter as of teeth, and then he was in the trench, following the wire and the sound.

In a shelf scratched from the earth, there was a thing with many arms and legs, something tall, crouched forward, its heads bowed, its bare skin goose-pimpled with cold. They couldn't feel the cold, Anne had told him.

From where he crouched, Ned couldn't tell its purpose, what it wanted, nor where it had come from, whether its stitches were Anne's work, or the work of an infernal Prussian, a brigade of Austrian Ingenieurs armed with bone saws. It might have been left behind by retreat, or pushed forward in advance. It might have once been French or Indian, or Canadian. It might be ANZAC or even American, but none of that was apparent when it lay pressed against the earth where it had dug half a den. It was dying. But. They were all dying, he thought, every last one.

"Hello," he said. "Are you awake?"

The sound it made was somewhere between a cry and a gasp. It lunged toward him, its limbs snapping and flailing. The bulky body could not move, and its weight restrained the creature's reach. It might already be dead, in parts. Anne had told him that some Talosites died body by body, the living flesh still grafted to the dead. Soon the creature withdrew to the mud cave, and the nest of its limbs, which coiled around its body.

"Can I help?" he asked, that being the only question he could think of that mattered.

The creature moaned. He felt through his pockets for the chocolate creams his mother had sent. Talosites didn't eat; they were fueled by mycological processes, not animal digestion. In Anne's words, they released enzymes that digested their own bodies. But he had seen them attracted by smell: the slit nose of a dog fluttering delicately where it protruded beneath the throat of a man.

He held out the chocolates. "Who made you?" he asked.

The creature moaned.

He unrolled his blanket and held it out. The creature's many eyes observed it, snatched it, and drew it close around some of its shoulders, then another long, articulated limb scooped up the chocolate.

"Stay here as long as you can," he said, "Stay quiet. They won't know if we don't tell them."

Then he climbed out, his back resolutely turned and his ears closed to the sounds the creature made as it ate his chocolate. He realized he was disobeying the orders of the War Office and Anne's own imperatives to find and to return these creatures to her, in whatever state he found them. He could not tell where his nausea came from: his own exhaustion, the dying creature in the trench, the fact of his own treason. But then in camp, alone, he walked down the line of tents and listened to the chatter, and the silence came to him easily, so he found a corner under damp canvas and slept.

THE LAST TIME he saw her she had built a creature from horse bones and men and wolves, from pigs inoculated before their execution, their tiny blue eyes looking disconsolately from human faces. She was railing against the state of the materials, complaining that the Germans always treated their dying with lazarites. She told him about the Beauchamps who should have pressed the issue with the War Office, and about Calloway's distaste for mass inoculation.

"Father thinks every soldier should be inoculated," she said. "Thought. I think so as well. He was working on a monograph when he died."

She was feverish, her left arm limp across his back, and her left hand restless in his. She shivered. It was the exhilarating march through the rains of October. They had an hour together.

"I can't see why anyone would resist it," she told him. "You understand the necessity, I'm sure."

"No," Ned said.

She sat up, pulled his rough coat around her shoulders.

"How can you possibly say that when it means you could be one of—" Here she hesitated. Us, he thought she was going to say, one of us, but she drew the word back into her mouth "—them forever and ever?"

"Is that what you want?"

She said nothing.

"Because." He paused a long moment. "I don't want it. I've signed away my life, but I don't think I signed away my afterlife."

"That's stupid," she said. "You should want to live on however long you can. Forever if you can. Forever and ever. You shouldn't want to go and leave anyone behind. Not ever."

Gently, he withdrew his arm from beneath her head.

5

ANNE

He stood up. Fool. Dressed. Fool fool. She unwound his overcoat from her shoulders, which was faintly warm, though always damp, and smelled of his sweat and his tobacco, his mud and his hands. She didn't tell him what she knew: that he was already teeming with lazarites, his whole body, that she'd probably transferred it to him the first time she kissed him. He might guess that.

He might not guess the truth, though. That once, while he slept, she had padded barefoot to her desk for a charm bag made of pig's skin, still supple with life, though it was long dead. She had upended it on her palm, the white dust of transformation, inherited from her father, the promise of return. As before she had dabbed it on John and Violet, here she dropped it on his lips and fingers, blowing filaments across his skin. She felt like the dark fairy at the christening, the one no one invited, who nevertheless arrived and changed the story.

She thought, he'll turn on the stair and come back to me. She thought, he'll pause in the hall and come back, while the pillow is still warm beside me. But then when she stood, she saw his familiar back, his slump, his steady, inexorable marching step setting out down the muddy road to Mons. But he'll come back when it's done. Next week, with some multifarious creature, something magnificent, then he will carry her up the stairs, and together—

O Ned, love: you've left, but you carry me with you forever and ever.

6

ANNE AND NED

I n October she was always cold. Her left hand grew weaker, the incision tender, as though it harboured some internal infection long after the skin healed. Every day she examined it for the red stain of sepsis beneath her skin.

THE DAY after his last day with her, inside her, the last day he felt any peace, or the stillness and comfort of her skin, he walked halfway to her billet. Lit a cigarette. Stopped. Turned around.

SHE COULD STILL FEEL Ned's kisses on her wrist. She wondered when he would return, if he had found any

Schellenberg automata to bring back to her. He'd followed the other Canadians she supposed, toward Mons. He would return when he could, and she found herself touching the bit of platinum wire that wrapped her finger, which she had so far neglected to throw into her workbox for use on a new creature. She chose not to care, focused instead on the work at hand: the collection and reintegration of Schellenberg Automata and her own Talosites. She marched eastward, over landscapes destroyed in 1914, without farms, nor brooks nor chestnut trees, just the names of towns, bellowing like trumpets from her old schoolbooks, so it was hard to work in the din of their history, rattling over the countryside with the galloping hooves of her own Sleipnirs.

Calloway rarely spoke, concerned with operations and orders, irrelevancies she hardly understood. She remained in the workroom, focused with the precision of a microscope on the seam between two bodies, the intersection of two entwining spinal columns, and the stitch she developed to bind dura matter to dura matter. So fine, now, that she worked it with a jeweller's eyepiece, and often found her back pulsating, then numb, as she crouched over bodies. She whispered to them, telling them of their futures and they offered their spines to her needle, as though they wanted the reunification she promised.

IT RAINED through the end of October, steady misery balanced by the exhilaration of real movement, finally, along old Roman roads and new Napoleonic routes lined with blasted chestnuts and plane trees. Ned saw the Fort Garry Horse take the day at le Cauteau. It was strange to ride and walk over open country after so long spent in the timeless and disorienting mud of various rivers and hills, lost villages, the stumps of trees, the remains of cellars, and the fallen chimney stones, the bones, and the matted fallen uniforms that were often all one saw of the long dead. He might almost forget that she—

ON THE RARE nights she slept long enough to dream, she saw the breakfast table and Bärchen advancing on the marmalade. Her father's right calf incised, retractors holding open the skin while the fluid of his sciatic nerve leaked into a vial that Calloway held, and she worked French knots and featherstitch over his ankle. Violet propped up in her little chair, grey-skinned. Outside, a thunderstorm and Millicent collecting abandoned croquet mallets, the guns of August, as they came to be known. Among the toast and coffee of the breakfast table, newspapers black with ink spelling three letters: W A R. Then Father tried to stand and fell, tearing the stitches. She mended his leg with blanket stitch and her perennial herring-

bone. "Anne," he said, "perhaps this will be the last."
Six eyes appraised her: Father's and Violet's and John's
in one body, their mouths working, but fallen silent.
She called out to Millicent, too, and said, "come now,
it's time. We'll begin with the vagus nerve in your
throat."

AN EVENING IN LATE OCTOBER, returning to the
regimental clearing station, he looked over a parapet
and saw, riding along the road, the men of Lord
Strathcona's Horse. He stopped to admire them, their
mounts, their easy demeanour. So much like knights,
he waved to them like a schoolboy, until he saw the
end of the column and his hand dropped to his side.
An eight-legged beast on a lead. Two more behind it,
also on leads, heads lowered, their long backs a patchwork of bay and grey and chestnut. As they drew
closer he stepped back, but could not stop staring at
their long, fluid strides, their human eyes, and
wonder who could ride a creature like that. After
them, other creatures: a heavy body, mostly horse
studded with human limbs. He could see Anne in the
neat seams, the careful balance she struck between
utility and horror, or beauty. He wondered if she had
slept, or if she had given up on such human necessi-
ties. Sleep. Food. Kisses. If all her hours were now
spent in jerry-rigged operating theatres, a needle

pinched between her fingers. He wondered if she had thought of him, however briefly, if she waited for his voice calling out to her from the courtyard.

CALLOWAY CAME AND WENT. So did Récamier. The orderlies appeared and disappeared as she requested things: an adult man with all limbs intact; a dead child whose tiny hands and juvenile nervous systems were more precious than any War Office Beauchamp would admit. She sent the orderly whose name she could not remember to fever hospitals filled with influenza patients. Perhaps he was Charles, or perhaps there were two Charles's. She couldn't say. Some of them disappeared, like Calloway did, and came back, but the Charleses were reliable, bringing children and girls, bringing soldiers warm with fever and red-streaked with sepsis. Following Schellenberg's precepts, she inoculated them before they died, in preparation for the transformation.

Once when Calloway saw her take delivery, he had objected.

"Do you think Father didn't inoculate me? When I had scarlet fever?" she asked. "I know he fed me lazarites."

He looked at her in a way she could not then name. Perhaps confusion. A kind of perplexed compassion.

"Anne, he didn't—"

She laughed. He was stupid sometimes. "Of course he did. Did you think he'd do otherwise?"

"How old were you?"

IN THE RAIN, Ned directed a stretcher-bearer to ignore the tangle of limbs—one of ours? Theirs?—twitching in the mud.

"Aren't we to—"

"—No."

"QUITE SMALL. SIX."

Calloway closed his eyes.

"Forgive me, Anne. I did not understand the depth of his—"

She waited. He did not continue. She prodded. "Forgive what?"

He walked away. It made her angry. She followed after, saying, "You know he didn't exclude himself from his experiments. Why would he exclude me? Do you think I would exclude John? Or Violet? Or Ned?"

NED STARTED. He'd heard something, a small voice, familiar. "What?" he asked. "You said—"

"—I didn't say anything, Sarge."

"Well then," Ned continued, "It isn't worth your life. It never was. They're already long dead."

Overhead, a flare.

"I saw it move, though. I saw it move."

The boy was eighteen. Ned offered him a cigarette.

"You will, sometimes. But it's dead, nonetheless. And we should leave the dead in peace."

"YOU KNOW what he told us. What he said in the monograph: All flesh has an afterlife. And from that perspective, are we not angels, ushering them from one form to the next?"

AT NIGHT the taste of hot tea in a metal cup, which had been the taste of her mouth the first time she kissed him. He would find her. When it was over. When they were all returned to the quiet of a grave, he would find her. Until then he couldn't think—

CALLOWAY STARED AT HER.

"First it was the croup, then the whooping cough," she said. She would have said more, but found the words failed in the heat of that memory: the last night, when she knew Violet was dying she had fetched the little pigskin bag Father had given her. She had not fed it as she ought, honey and blood, so there was so little to transfer to Violet's tongue, her eyes, hoping that it would have time enough to propagate through Violet's body, imagining its spread, the webs it would form beneath her skin, as it had formed around her father's body in the privacy of his grave. She would be wrapped safe and tight beside him. Cold, yes, but not gone. Only waiting.

NOVEMBER 11 and Ned was behind what had been a garden wall; their advance arrested by the news from Compiègne, he loitered near what had been the front line in Ville-sur-Haine outside Mons. Looking northeast he could imagine them, the huge creatures of German imperial invention, waiting for their advance and the inevitable clash with the huge creatures of Anne's invention. The clock counted inexorably forward. His eyes have closed in the bright light of morning after another sleepless night, he thought he could see them on the horizon line, the hulking masses of flesh and eyes, taller than cathedrals, outlined in the mist that stretched from the front line (which had also been the front of 1914) as far east as he could imagine, and all of it full of Anne's children, stitching themselves together into larger and stranger bodies, looming and scrambling through the wet morning. He wondered what they saw, whether they looked back at the realms of the living and wanted to return, to unstitch themselves and walk home on two feet, or whether—having once crossed the line into death— they were a different kind of creature now. Something made of platinum and the ichor of horses, bound by Anne's vision and her needlework. He wondered if anyone, ever, had asked them what they wanted.

WORD CAME from Compiègne but she ignored it. She needed more horses. She needed young women. She needed more pigs. Herds of pigs, farms of pigs, whole worlds of piglets, with their tiny eyes and soft pink snouts. She needed the skeletons of whales brought in from the channel beaches. She needed blood and gold wire. Outside her windows, the orderlies waited at the gate, as though anything could ever change, but in the decayed world around the villa she saw nothing but materials with which to build: stone and brick, earthworms and larks and the cosmopolitan rats of no-man's-land, her own body, and Récamier's, and that of the men standing by the road, waiting for news.

For weeks she had ignored the War Office when the Beauchamps visited, and all of them had complied with her requests because this was the final push, and on the other side of their eastward advance she could hear the Deutsches Reich collapsing into its constituent parts, the Schellenberg Automata she saw were pitiful things, beaten in the advance. Nevertheless, she needed them.

She looked down at her watch, blood-caked like her nails. It was 10.58.

BEHIND HIM, the Belgian nurse shouted, *"Fais attention!"*

10.59. A report reverberating over stone. On the ground now, he wondered if he would awaken to find himself on the other side of the line, a body among other bodies. Thousands of bodies. Millions. He wished he could tell her not to. He wished—

"Oh," he said, looking up through the grey sky, "this is a bloody stupid—

THE TALOSITE

All through November they came home, trailing wire where they had been torn from one another, or escaped their captors. In the mornings she often found they had recollected themselves, rewired the severed limbs, re-stitched the sutures, both hers and those made by the clumsier Ingenieurs up and down the line. In November, the battlefields nominally abandoned, the Schellenberg Automata surrendered, they arrived on carts and walking in parade, chained together by various limbs. She ignored orders. She brought them in, and instead of dismantling them and sending them up the line with detailed reports of their dissections, she brought them home, too.

Calloway, mute and compliant, maintained the batteries, and the orderlies came and went, and no one spoke anymore.

In the weeks before and after the Armistice, Anne understood them in a way she had not before, though they remained silent except for the occasional gibber and roar, or single words from mouths still linked with functional brains that said, perhaps, *mütterchen* or *no*. More than anything they wanted to return to one another, regardless of their original loyalties. When they came home to her, by night often, ignoring the orders of daytime and emerging from the chaos of troop trains and surrenders, she said, "I'm glad to see you have come home, my dears." When they brought her their fragments, she reunited them. But her greatest and loveliest innovation was not what she did for them, but when she taught them to stitch limb to limb to limb themselves, so that they might continue the Great Reunification without her.

Sometimes, at dawn, she saw them leave again, whole as they hadn't been before, and she wondered where they went, creeping and striding into the mist of November. Sometimes Calloway stood by her, but his countenance registered no understanding. It hurt her to see them go, but she understood their impulse.

Then, one morning Calloway was gone too, and she didn't recognize the orderlies who clustered in the drawing room. Then Beauchamp—or, not Beauchamp, someone like Beauchamp. It didn't matter. There were a million Beauchamps.

"Where is Ned?" she asked.

"Ned? I don't know Ned."

"Récamier?"

"He left last week."

"Calloway?"

"Gone home."

He had tried to talk to her. She had said nothing.

The most recent Schellenberg Automaton whined at her feet. It was civilian and wolf, she had determined, small and light. She stroked its head until it quieted.

"It's time for you to go home, as well."

"I thought there'd be another letter from Doktor Schellenberg. He's never written anything about sentient automata. About what happens when they begin to spontaneously—"

"Miss Markham. Listen to me."

Her fingers were damp with fluid weeping from the clumsy seam along the creature's throat. She meant to re-stitch it, something neat and flexible, but there was so much to do.

"Dr. Schellenberg was shot trying to escape from the camp in Islington."

"Oh," she said. "Well, we'll have to find him, then. I hope he hasn't been cremated. In the meantime I shall stay here."

"We've already begun destroying—"

Then, even Beauchamp—or not-Beauchamp—stopped himself, as though he understood the awfulness of what he said.

"Come with me," she said.

She led him down through the kitchen, and out through the little door that must once have led to a kitchen garden, past what had once been walls against what had once been espaliered apricots and peaches. The wolf-creature followed them out to the barn, then the field beyond that, where the orderlies never went.

Her last count had been twenty-three discrete Talosites, but more had arrived overnight. Most were hers, come home again, but she saw so many others as well. This one with sixteen heads and as many spines, a long centipede-shape, now curled around a surveillance giant she had built in July. The two nestled together like littermates.

"Ned?" she asked. "Ned?" None of them turned any of their heads. They never did.

"Anne. The war is over. Your work here is done. We must put them to rest, and you must come home."

"Rest?" she asked, amused. "They're coming home. This very minute they're coming home."

"They're—" He began. "How many?"

"Twenty, thirty," she said.

"No. How many men—"

The question was stupid, and it took her a moment to think. "Thousands," she said. "At least. Tens of thousands. More. And there will only be more and more as they come home."

She reached out one hand to touch a skull. She could see through the skin to the tracks that bullets made in brains. It was still Talosite, though, despite the damage done before and after its human death. That was the beauty of the system she had dreamed. She wondered if Schellenberg would—

"—Miss Markham." The voice sharp, strangled, as Calloway's voice had often seemed since the last push. Where had Calloway gone?

"He's gone home," Beauchamp said, and she was surprised to learn she had asked the question aloud. If she was a Talosite, she would not wonder, because the most essential communication—the communications of pleasure and pain, of sensation and observation and insight—those would all happen inside a body that grew with each death until everyone was here, coming home. If you wanted to know anything, anything at all, you would only have to wait for the right mind to join you.

"We're going to bring you home, too."

Home. What a word to use. Home.

"Captain Beauchamp—"

"—My name is Cholmondeley. I replaced Beauchamp in August—"

"—It doesn't matter, of course. They don't have names."

"Miss Markham. The war is over."

She could have laughed.

"Look at them," she said, "look at them all. Is the war really over?"

"What do you—what does that—"

"—the living ones will be demobbed and carry it

home, every last one of them who's been sunk in the mud. All the hospitals are full of it, I imagine. All of France and Belgium—some corner of a foreign field is forever Armillaria lazarites. And it grows so quickly once one is dead. It covers us over and make us into something. It will be all over the world now, the Great War's real victor. Can you think of anything more fitting?"

Instead of answering, he ruffled his hair with long fingers. She thought, if he was one of mine, in a hospital, breathing his last breaths, I would take those long fingers and put them to work. I would augment his nerves with platinum and iridium. I would bind him tightly to the spines of a hundred other men. A thousand. I would build a Talosite as tall as a cathedral spire, and we would walk home together, him, and me, and Ned and Calloway, all walk home together across the channel, down the streets of London, a magnificent creature, tall as the Colossues of Rhodes, patchwork skin, furred and feathered and smooth and rough, all stitched together with meticulous stitches, into this remarkable and lovely creature, taller than St Paul's. And it would be only the first of many, a parade of giants, walking on long and beautiful limbs made of all the fallen horses and children and men and women, all the nurses and VADs and Sikh corporals and Canadian farmers and Bavarian counts. We could all come home.

"We don't need them. Let them die, Miss

Markham. Please. They've served their time. There's no need to prolong their suffering."

"Suffering," she said. "How little you understand, Captain Beauchamp."

To that he had no response. In the silence that followed, Anne considered possibilities. Then she said, "I suppose I'm the only one left who speaks the language." She covered her eyes as though she was crying, and the Beauchamp fled, saying "I will be back soon."

She didn't have long. Ten minutes. Fifteen before he organized the removal of her lab, she supposed, and in the meantime she had said she would collect her things. Maybe her notebooks, as a pretence. As she stacked them she considered the next steps: out into the passage again, listening carefully for the noise on the lower floor as the Beauchamp-type's men searched the house, turning over the surgical theatre and disordering her needles and her platinum.

But her plans were in place. The Talosites and the Schellenberg Automata were coming home to her, all of them, ready to combine and recombine, and then —when they were so magnificent, they could no longer be denied—they would march in a triumphal column, into all the cities of the war, where people waited for them.

In the long hall outside her room she listened. A crash. Heavy boots in and out of doorways, down the corridor past the kitchen, to the basement where the bodies were waiting for their next transformation, and on her egress, she took the briefest of moments to send her apologies that they, too, could not go with her, but must continue on the path of all flesh.

Down the long corridor to the little salon with the tall windows, the footsteps behind her, now carrying boxes away, her records, perhaps, her diagrams. They'd be hidden in some secret library where they would be of no good to anyone. Until they were needed again, she supposed, for some other undertaking of war or empire.

In the garden, through the darkness to the hedge where she found the gap she was looking for and slipped out to the far fields where they were sleeping. She thought she saw eight now, or ten, more arriving in the darkness, as though they sensed the gathering. In the darkness they fit themselves together, limbs threading into limbs, fingers further knotting the webs she had knit of skin and nerve, until the whole of them were connected, bound to one another in body and mind. She found her way up, climbing over limbs and backs and heads, who seemed to welcome her presence, until she found an ear. She didn't know if anything would hear her, but she whispered into it, "It's time to go, dear. We should be gone long before dawn, back east across the battlefields. We'll travel by night. By day we'll sleep in a cathedral if we can, or a castle. We'll find the others, and we will go home together." Perhaps they'd visit Neuve-Chapelle, before that, and eventually the little stone in the churchyard where she had left Violet, the larger stone near it where father lay beside his only grandchild. In the dark, their bodies colonized by the interlocking white veils of lazarites and waiting for the last trump, when the dead rise incorruptible and all the lost are reunited.

She felt its strength gather beneath her, and miraculously it stood. She caressed a hand and a foot, a head and a back, and together they set off. She could hear through the conjoined bodies the rhythms of a hundred thousand hearts.

ACKNOWLEDGEMENTS

Thanks, first, to Michael Kelly and Undertow Publications. Then to the friends who talked and listened: Tegan Moore, Dave Hickey, Sarah Ervine, Sean Henry, Christine Neulieb. Finally, my family: Don and David, Sharron, Dave, Paulette, and Ian.

ABOUT THE AUTHOR

Rebecca Campbell is a Canadian writer of weird stories and climate change fiction. Her work has appeared in *The Year's Best Science Fiction, The Year's Best Science Fiction and Fantasy, The Year's Best Dark Fantasy and Horror,* and *The Best Science Fiction of the Year, Volumes 5 & 6,* in addition to many contemporary magazines, including *The Magazine of Fantasy and Science Fiction, Clarkesworld,* and *Interzone.* She won the Sunburst award for short fiction in 2020 for "The Fourth Trimester is the Strangest" and the Theodore Sturgeon Memorial Award in 2021 for "An Important Failure." NeWest Press published her first novel, *The Paradise Engine,* in 2013. You can find her online at whereishere.ca.